One Night Stand

By Cindy Kirk

ONE NIGHT STAND
WHEN SHE WAS BAD

One Night Stand

CINDY KIRK

AVON

An Imprint of HarperCollinsPublishers

AVON BOOKS
An Imprint of HarperCollins*Publishers*
10 East 53rd Street
New York, New York 10022-5299

Copyright © 2008 by Cindy Kirk
ISBN-13: 978-0-7394-9662-6

Printed in the U.S.A.

To my wonderful editor, Erika Tsang, who gently pushes me to reach my highest potential. Thank you for your insightful comments and suggestions. Most of all, thank you for caring!

To my agents, Annelise Robey and Christina Hogrebe . . . I don't know what I'd do without you guys. You're the best!

To my daughter, Wendy. You've always been my staunchest champion. Thank you for all your love and support.

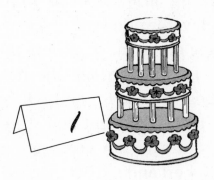

"*Everyone knows the best one night stands* happen at weddings." From the dais, Marcee Robbens scanned the room.

No expense had been spared in decorating the ballroom of the large downtown Chicago hotel for the reception. The crystal chandeliers glittered like a thousand diamonds, and the candles at each of the linen-clad tables cast a romantic glow. Tropical flowers flown in especially for the evening were everywhere and their enticing fragrance filled the air.

Marcee inhaled deeply and felt a tingle of excitement skitter up her spine. "There's nothing like being all dressed up with a hotel room only an elevator ride away," she added. "I've been counting down the days until this event."

Jenny Marshall, the new bride and Marcee's best friend, threw back her head and laughed. "Here I thought you were making those X's on your calendar because you couldn't wait to see Robert and me get married."

"It was a fabulous wedding," Marcee said quickly, knowing that was an understatement. Every detail had been planned to perfection, even the unscripted moments, it seemed. Like the look in Robert's eyes when he'd seen Jenny start down the aisle. It had all been there, the love, the devotion, and the promise . . .

Marcee's heart twisted and she let her gaze drop to the champagne glass. She'd once dreamed of finding such a man for herself, but in her world, good men were as hard to find as a pair of comfortable stilettos.

Swallowing a sigh, she returned her attention to her friend. Jenny's face glowed with happiness, and Marcee fought a pang of envy. "You're a beautiful bride, Jen."

If it were *her* wedding day, she knew she would have taken the compliment and run with it. But Jenny waved the words aside and cast an admiring gaze at her black chiffon. "You're the one who is beautiful. That dress looks like it was designed with you in mind."

Marcee didn't argue. The slinky maid-of-honor dress had been a definite hit. Last fall, when Jenny told her she could choose any dress—as long as it was cocktail length and black—Marcee's interest in being part of the wedding had spiked. She'd spent days scouring the shops along Michigan Avenue searching for a dress that possessed the "Wow" factor. When she walked down the aisle, she'd wanted every man in the church to say, "Wow, I want her."

There had been plenty such looks on her trek to the altar. At least one of those men *had* to be interested in acting on that desire. Marcee slid her tongue across her lips and pondered the possibilities. She knew what she wanted. Broad shoulders. Rock hard abs. Tight butt. Big—

"Marcee?"

She pulled her thoughts away from delicious, delectable men and cast a sideways glance at her friend.

"We probably won't have another chance to talk privately tonight," Jenny said, her eyes dark and intense. "There's something I've wanted to say to you for a long time."

Marcee shifted in her seat, not sure what to make of her friend's suddenly solemn expression.

"You know how I feel about Robert. And I'd never have met him if you hadn't made me go out that night." Jenny's voice grew thick with emotion. "Thank you for giving me the love of my life."

The same look she'd seen in Robert's gaze was now in Jenny's eyes. So much love . . .

For a second Marcee felt as if she'd taken a punch to the heart. Her breath caught in her throat. Tears sprang to her eyes. But she quickly rallied, blinking back the moisture, hoping Jenny hadn't noticed her momentary loss of composure.

Out of the corner of her eye Marcee saw Robert returning to the table. She leaned over and gave Jenny a heartfelt hug. "You two are going to have a wonderful life."

"Because of you," Jenny murmured.

The tears Marcee had banished only moments before returned to press against her lids. "No." She swallowed past the lump in her throat. "Because you were willing to seize the day."

"Mrs. Marshall." Robert's smoldering gaze fixed on his wife. "Would you care to dance with your husband?"

Marcee released her hold on her friend and rose

to her feet. She gave Jenny a wink and stepped aside. By the look in Robert's eye, he had far more than dancing on his mind.

Jenny took her husband's hand, her smile blinding, and Marcee fought a pang of envy. Still, knowing her friend was right where she needed to be made it easy for her to concentrate on her own enjoyment guilt-free.

Marcee shifted her thoughts to the evening ahead, anticipation fueling her steps. It was definitely time to get this party started. But she'd barely gone ten feet when she was waylaid by Jenny's teenage sister, Annie, and her friend Fern.

"Marcee, you look incredible." Fern stared in open admiration.

"I wish Mom would've let me wear something like that," Annie said with a pout.

Marcee smoothed the skirt with the palm of her hand. Not only did the dress show off her curves to full advantage, it displayed some serious skin. Sexy but tastefully elegant was how the clerk had described it. She hadn't cared about anything other than the sexy part. Thanks to running four miles a day, at thirty-two she still had slender, toned thighs and a firm derriere. Her perky breasts were large enough to capture a man's interest. Speaking of which . . .

As fun as talking to two teenagers could be, she had more important things on her mind. She let her gaze sweep the room. "Aren't there any single guys here?"

Fern and Annie giggled.

"My dad is here somewhere," Fern said. "I could introduce you."

"That's okay." The last thing Marcee wanted was to hang out with anyone's *father*. "I'll see you later."

Waving a quick good-bye, she grabbed a glass of champagne from a tuxedoed waiter with a silver tray and took a sip. The bubbly tickled her nose, and her already high spirits soared.

Salsa music filled the air, and while Marcee rolled her eyes at the sight of the conservative accountant types moving in time to the sexy Latin beat, the rhythm *was* intoxicating. It wasn't long until *her* hips began to sway.

She danced her way across the room, stopping several times to chat with friends. But then the rhythm would call her name and she'd start moving again.

She was halfway across the ballroom when she saw the little boy sitting alone at a round linen-clad table. No name came immediately to mind but she had the feeling they'd been introduced.

The bow tie at his neck was askew and the tail of his white shirt partially pulled out of the waistband. His hair looked like he'd just raked his fingers through the blond strands.

The boy's full, perfectly sculpted lips turned downward in a sad frown, and though she couldn't be positive, it looked as if he had tears in his eyes. Her heart clenched. She'd planned to dance on by but at the last minute found herself pulling out a chair and sitting down beside him. "Are you okay?"

His lower lip wobbled and two tears dropped down his cheek. Marcee fought a surge of helplessness. While she prided herself on her ability to handle almost any situation, she threw up the white flag on this one.

"I want my mommy," the boy wailed, giving a not-so-gentle tug on her dress.

"Don't touch." Marcee pried his pudgy fingers from the delicate chiffon and softened her words with a smile.

Still, the child's eyes widened at the firm tone. He lifted his gaze, his eyes large and very blue. "I sorry."

Marcee suddenly realized why the kid looked so

familiar. He'd been the ring bearer. She struggled to remember his name. "Your name is Adam, right?"

He shook his head.

Damn. Still, she was sure it started with an A. "Austin?"

This time he shook his head from side to side and giggled as if the attempt to discover his name was some sort of game.

Marcee felt her patience start to fray. "Abercrombie?"

The boy's giggle turned to a peal of laughter. "Andrew," he said, holding up three fingers. "I three."

That's right. Little Andrew. Named after his father, Big Andrew. It was a good thing his dad wasn't named Dick, she thought. The kid would probably be traumatized for life.

"Are you having fun?" Marcee asked, desperately looking around for reinforcements.

It was a simple question, but the second the boy's face scrunched up, she knew she should have kept her mouth shut.

"I want my mommy." His voice grew louder and more shrill with each word. "I want my mommy now."

Marcee recoiled against the back of her chair.

"Hey, buddy." A dark-haired man who must

have been walking by stooped down next to the boy. "Something wrong?"

Marcee's breath caught in her throat, and the tension that had gripped her only moments before was replaced with a rush of adrenaline. Now this was more like it . . .

The man's hair was the color of rich mahogany, cut stylishly short but with just enough length for a woman to run her fingers through. Some might consider his eyes to be brown, but Marcee's discerning gaze saw gold in the hazel depths.

She was almost a hundred percent sure this handsome hunk wasn't Big Andrew. The kid's parents had been at the rehearsal dinner last night. And while they'd been at opposite ends of a very long table, Marcee knew she would have noticed this man, no matter where he was seated.

Classically handsome would be how her friend Jenny would describe the guy. Hot and delectable were the two words that popped immediately into her own mind.

"I want my mommy." The kid's lower lip jutted out and his hands clenched into small fists at his side.

The determined glint in his eyes reminded Marcee of herself during that critical time of the month when she wanted—no, needed—chocolate.

The man's curious gaze settled on her.

Marcee held out her hands and shrugged. "He's possessed by demons."

"I take it he's not yours." His eyes gleamed with good humor.

"Nope." She shook her head. "No husband."

He flashed a mouthful of perfect white teeth. "Me, either."

Marcee raised a brow.

"I mean, no wife."

"I-want-my-mommy." The boy slipped off the chair and immediately stomped his foot.

"Watch," Marcee said in a conspiratorial whisper. "In a minute he's going to start spewing green bile."

The guy grinned. "Maybe it's time to go looking for the she-devil who spawned him."

"I know the she-devil . . . er, his mother." Marcee grabbed the child's shirt before he could dart away. "I should take him to her."

She hesitated, reluctant to leave.

"Sam McKelvey." He held out his hand, his gaze firmly fixed on her. "Once you make your delivery, would you be interested in a . . . drink?"

Marcee tightened her one-handed hold on the squirming boy and took Sam's hand in hers with the other.

"Marcee Robbens," she said in a low husky voice. "And I'm definitely interested."

She let her hand linger an extra beat. Something flared in his eyes, and an answering flutter caused a tightening low in her belly.

"Andrew Michael, you are in big trouble." A brunette with short permed hair stood next to the table, hands on ample hips, eyes shooting blue fire.

Marcee breathed a sigh of relief. She couldn't remember the last time she'd been so happy to see Jenny's nosy cousin, Mary Lou. "I thought you might be looking for him," she said.

"One minute he was by my side, the next he was gone." Mary Lou shifted her gaze to the wide-eyed boy and pursed her lips. "I've been looking for you for almost fifteen minutes."

Andrew batted his long lashes. "I sorry, Mommy."

"You should be." Though Mary Lou glanced at Sam, instead of assuaging her obvious curiosity she scooped Andrew into her arms. "The flower girl's father is waiting. He wants to get some pictures of the two of them together."

"Good luck," Marcee said. "I'm no expert, but little Andrew doesn't seem in the picture taking mood to me."

For the first time, Mary Lou appeared to notice her son's mutinous expression. Her arms tightened around him. "Maybe if I hurry we can get one or two decent shots. Thanks for watching him, Marcee. I owe you."

With the squirming boy clasped tightly in her arms, Mary Lou hurried off, heels clicking on the hardwood floor.

"Looks like you've done your good deed for the day," Sam said, a twinkle in his eye.

"I have and now it's your turn." Marcee unwrapped one of the chocolate kisses scattered across the tabletop, popped it into her mouth and held out her hand. "Dance with me."

For what seemed like forever, but in actuality was probably only a handful of heartbeats, Sam hesitated. "I have to warn you, I'm not much of a dancer."

She reached down, grabbed his hand and pulled him to his feet. "No worries. I'll lead."

He chuckled and pulled her close. The spicy scent of his aftershave and the warmth of his body stirred her senses. Slowly they began to move in time to the music. They fit together perfectly and the sudden intimacy of the moment took Marcee by surprise.

"We're not on the dance floor," she murmured, resting her head against his chest.

"That doesn't matter to me, and I don't think you care," he said in that deep voice of his. "I have the feeling we're alike in that respect."

Marcee didn't answer. His arms were strong, his chest broad, and it had been six long months since she'd been in a man's arms. An eternity by any measure.

Her eyelids drifted shut and she lost herself in the not-to-be-forgotten feel of a muscular body pressed against hers. And not just *any* body. There was something about Sam. He exuded a kind of solid strength that she found appealing.

But before she let herself get too interested, there were a couple things she needed to check out first. He'd said he wasn't married, but he could still be attached. Her heart gave a ping at the thought.

Mentally crossing her fingers, Marcee leaned back in his arms so she could see his reaction. "Do you have a girlfriend?"

The look of surprise on his face was too spontaneous to be faked. "I wouldn't be dancing with you if I did."

Marcee released the breath she'd been holding and her heart did a happy dance.

"How about you?" he asked.

"Single. No current boyfriend. Never married."

"I was married . . . once." Though his tone gave nothing away, something in his eyes told her he hadn't wanted the split.

"How long have you been divorced?" Marcee asked softly.

"We didn't divorce," he said. "She died."

"I'm sorry," Marcee murmured. It seemed inadequate but she didn't know what else to say. She couldn't imagine falling in love only to have them die at such a young age. "Any children?"

"One daughter." Pride filled his eyes. "She's spending the night with a friend."

Though Sam tossed the statement out there all casual and offhand, Marcee's heart skipped a beat. Whether he realized it or not, he'd let her know he was free until the morning.

Marcee slid her hand up his back and her fingers into his short dark hair.

"How about you?" He tilted his head back into her touch. "Any children?"

Marcee shook her head. "Nope."

"Parenthood is great," he said. "I wouldn't trade my daughter for anything."

"How old is she?"

"Seventeen," he said.

"Months?"

"Years."

A teenager. This handsome hunk had a daughter in high school . . . unbelievable. Marcee widened her eyes. "How old were you when she was born? Twelve?"

Sam chuckled. "Close. I was nineteen."

Marcee tried to remember what she'd been doing at that age. In college. Working two jobs. It might not have been the good life, but she'd still tried to make it fun.

"Enough about me." His gaze lingered on her face for a long moment. "You're an attractive woman. How come there's no husband and children in the picture?"

"No maternal instincts," Marcee said, keeping her tone light. "And too many Mr. Wrongs."

"Those men were fools," he said.

Her heart warmed at his indignant tone. "You're very sweet."

His gaze met hers and her breath caught in her throat. Waves of testosterone rolled off him and over her, stirring her senses. He was so obviously male. So blatantly sexy. So completely desirable.

She dropped her gaze to his lips and time stood still. Though it was commonly understood that the man should make the first move, Marcee had never been good at following rules. She laid her palms flat on his chest and gave into temptation.

He tasted like champagne and wedding cake, a combination that suddenly seemed wildly erotic. For a second he hesitated and she worried he might push her away. Then his tongue teased the fullness of her lower lip, coaxing her to open to him, sweeping inside when she did.

Her entire body quivered. It was familiar, this flare of heat, the quick rush of hunger, yet at the same time . . . different.

When he released her, Marcee's head was spinning. "Wow," was all she could manage.

The dimple in his cheek flashed and her heart skipped a beat. The reception had started off a bit rocky but had definitely picked up. And now, staring into Sam's hazel eyes, Marcee realized that the best was yet to come.

2

The hotel room temperature was set at a pleasant seventy-four degrees, yet Marcee had been shivering ever since she and Sam had crossed the threshold. With anticipation? Or apprehension? Sam McKelvey certainly wasn't like any other man she'd known.

When he'd offered to walk her to her hotel room after the reception ended, she thought she knew what was on his mind. But when they reached her door, he gave her a kiss on the cheek, said something about being happy he'd met her, then turned and left.

She'd been so shocked that he made it halfway

down the hall before she rallied, calling him back. Then she gave him her prettiest smile and invited him in for a glass of wine.

She'd expected him to make his move the second he stepped into the room. But he followed her to the cabinet by the bed and discussed the merits of domestic versus imported wine while she opened the bottle and poured them each a glass.

Still trying to steer the situation in the direction she wanted it go, Marcee had moved to the love seat, deliberately leaving space beside her. He sat on the adjacent sofa instead.

Now poised on the edge of a floral cushion, with shoulders as stiff as any military man, Sam looked ready to bolt. She had no doubt once he finished his glass of wine he'd be gone.

Unless she changed his mind . . .

Marcee prided herself on her ability to get a man hot and bothered. A look, a smile, a sultry laugh was usually all it took. But this situation was different. It wasn't that Sam wasn't interested. She could see the desire in his eyes. No, the problem was his refusal to act on that need and her uncharacteristic reluctance to push him.

You're not good enough.

Marcee immediately shoved the ridiculous

thought aside even though she acknowledged it may have partially been the reason she'd kept her clothes on. Sam was a quality guy, obviously not prone to jumping in and out of bed with someone he'd just met.

While his self-control was part of his appeal, it only underscored the difference between them.

The crazy thing was, she found herself wanting to sleep with him not just because he was available and cute, but because she genuinely liked him. While he wasn't the best dancer, she'd had fun whirling across the hardwood floor in his arms. She'd also enjoyed talking with him. She couldn't remember the last time she'd connected so fully with someone. Of course after tonight, she'd probably never see him again . . .

"Why the frown?" Sam asked. "Is something wrong?"

Marcee's head jerked up. "Everything is great."

The look in his eyes said he wasn't convinced. "It's probably hard," he said, twisting the stem of the wineglass back and forth between his fingers, "watching your best friend get married and leave."

It was something she'd avoided thinking about ever since Jenny announced her engagement.

Though Marcee was happy for the new bride and groom, Jenny now had a new best friend—her husband.

"We'll still spend time together. After all, she and Robert will live right here in Chicago. She—" Marcee stopped the ridiculous babble. Who was she kidding? Certainly not Sam, to judge by the sympathetic look on his face. "Yeah, it'll be different."

Sam paused as if expecting her to continue, but Marcee wasn't into baring her soul. "We all get lonely sometimes. I imagine you do, too, what with your wife gone and all."

"I don't have time to think about it," Sam said with a shrug. "On the job, I'm totally focused on whatever case I'm investigating. By the time I finish for the day, work out, and eat, it's late. I collapse into bed, only to wake up and do the same thing all over again the next day."

Investigating? Marcee pulled her brows together. "Are you a P.I.?"

"I'm a police officer."

"Really?" She didn't know why she hadn't realized that. The close attention Sam paid to his surroundings and his blatant masculinity had been obvious clues.

"Actually, I'm a detective with the Chicago PD."

Sam slid a finger slowly up the side of his wineglass, and an answering shiver traveled up Marcee's skin.

"Does that change anything?" His finger continued its uphill journey, and Marcee's mouth went dry.

"Change anything?" she said finally when his finger came to a stop, unable to keep from imagining how it would feel if he'd slid that finger against certain sensitive parts of her anatomy.

"Most women don't like to hang out with cops," he said, his gaze watchful.

Was there a hint of challenge in his tone? It didn't matter. He'd given her an opening, and she was taking it. Marcee rose, took a step and dropped down beside him. Leaning close, she moved her lips to his ear.

"Haven't you figured it out yet?" she asked in a sultry whisper. "I'm not most women."

A dimple she didn't even know he had flashed in his cheek. He chuckled. "I'm beginning to realize that."

She scooted next to him and exhaled a satisfied sigh. Finally she was right where she wanted to be.

He slanted a sideways glance, his eyes more green than hazel in the light. "What is it you do?" he asked. "For a living, I mean."

"I'm a CPA. For D and D."

Since he was from Chicago, she didn't need to say more. The Dodson & Dodson accounting firm was well known in the region.

"An accountant?" His lips twitched and he glanced at her chest. "Where's your pocket protector?"

"Ha ha," Marcee said. "I've never heard that one before."

"Sorry." Sam shot her a wink. "Couldn't resist."

"Yeah, right." Marcee tried a stern voice but his teasing smile made it impossible.

"Seriously," he said, angling his body to face her. "How do you like being a CPA?"

To Marcee's surprise, he sounded as if he was truly interested, instead of simply marking time until he got her in bed. The thought both pleased and distressed her.

"I've always had a thing for numbers," she said, giving the question more thought than it probably deserved. "And I enjoy the clients. But lately I've felt as if I've fallen into a rut and can't get out."

In her heart, she knew that the time had come to leave D&D. But she hadn't been able to cut the tie. Maybe because she'd been there since college and it was the one stable thing in her life. Maybe because her coworkers were like family; a dysfunctional family, but a family nonetheless. Or maybe it was because she was thirty-two years old and still hadn't figured out what she really wanted out of life.

"When the time is right to leave, you'll know," he said.

Something in his tone told her he'd struggled with the same issue.

"Sounds like your job is all-consuming," she said. "Ever consider moving on?"

Sam took a sip of wine and his eyes took on a faraway look. "I think we all reach a point in our life where we step back and ask ourselves if we're where we should be."

Marcee noticed he hadn't answered her question. "Would you consider quitting the force?" she asked again, pinning him with her gaze.

His lips lifted in a slight smile. "If you're looking for a career change, I think you could have a great future in interrogation."

Marcee smiled. "Answer the question, Detective McKelvey."

"The thought has crossed my mind," Sam admitted. "In another year my daughter will be away at college. I haven't been much of a father to her. If I'm going to make up for those lost years, it's now or never."

While most of her conversations with men tended to be on the superficial side, Marcee found herself enjoying the depth of this one. "Would you get out of law enforcement altogether?"

"Probably not." He leaned back against the sofa cushion, appearing relaxed and no longer in a hurry to leave. "I'm looking at several options, including moving to a small town where the pace would be slower."

He might as well have waved a red flag in front of a bull. Though Marcee told herself what Sam did was none of her concern, small town life was one of her hot buttons.

"If you want my advice, don't do it," she said. "Believe me, such a life may seem idyllic but it definitely has a dark side."

Sam placed his glass on the table. "Dark side?"

"Very dark," Marcee said, her thoughts drifting back to her high school years. "If you're a teenager, there's nothing for you to do except drink, do drugs, or have sex."

Contrary to what the people in town had believed, she had avoided the drugs and the sex. But she had been on a first name basis with "Bud."

"Drinking, drugs, and sex?" Sam grimaced before a hopeful glint filled his eyes. "What about participating in sports? Aren't there more opportunities? Not just for boys but for girls . . . "

He continued to elaborate on the possibilities, and Marcee found herself drawn into a debate of the pros and cons of small town life. However, after several minutes her interest waned and she found herself focusing more on Sam's lips and the passion in his voice than on the words. She couldn't remember the last time she'd been so captivated by a man. And he hadn't even taken his clothes off . . .

Impulsively, she gave his forearm a bump with her elbow. "If we're going to spend all night talking, at least put your arm around me."

He chuckled and slipped his arm around her shoulders, letting his hand dangle down until it hovered just above her right breast.

Now this was more like it . . .

"What did you dislike most?" His dangling fingers played with the spaghetti strap of her dress.

She shivered as his thumb brushed against the bare skin just inside the dress's scooped neck. Her breast strained against the fabric, eagerly anticipating his touch. "I, um . . . "

What was there about this man that fired her senses and reduced her to a blithering idiot?

"The gossip," she blurted when the tip of his finger brushed against her nipple. "Everybody's always into their neighbor's business."

"People are concerned—"

"If there isn't any juicy news to spread, they make it up."

Sam's hand pulled back and he blew out a breath. "I've had others tell me the same thing."

"And if you move to a small town, it won't just be your daughter they'll be watching," Marcee warned. "They'll have their binoculars trained on you as well."

Sam silently absorbed her words. "Do you go home much?"

"Never!" Marcee snapped. Family was another of her hot buttons.

His eyes widened, and she realized by her quick response she'd opened the door to a whole lot of questions she'd rather not answer.

"Not often," she hastened to add. "I have too much going on in my own life, too many demands on my time."

"I'm sure you do." Admiration lit Sam's eyes and echoed in his voice. And when his gaze lingered, she had the feeling he was one of the few who could see the woman beneath the sexy body and brash facade. "I bet there's not much you can't handle."

"If something needs to be done, I do it myself." Marcee kept her tone deliberately light. "I may not be able to rely on anyone else, but Marcee always comes through for me."

Though she'd spoken in a joking manner, his brows pulled together. "Surely you don't believe you can only depend on yourself?"

She smiled. That's exactly what she was saying. Anyone she'd ever loved had disappointed her. Now, even Jenny had abandoned her . . .

Still, she wasn't asking for pity. She hadn't let the past hold her back, and she hadn't used it as an excuse. She'd made her own way and was a stronger woman because of the adversity.

"We've talked about me long enough," Marcee said. "Let's talk about you. Tell me why you agreed to come in for a drink."

"I enjoy your company," he said as if the answer was obvious. "I didn't want the evening to end."

"You enjoyed kissing me," Marcee reminded him. "Yet your lips haven't touched mine since you've walked through that door."

His gaze raked over her and a spray of goose bumps pebbled her skin.

"I like you, Marcee," he said. "But I know if I kissed you again, I wouldn't want to stop. Hell, one kiss and I wanted to take you right there in the ballroom with everyone watching."

The image brought a smile to Marcee's lips. "And that would have been a problem . . . why?"

"Public indecency?"

"The downside of hanging with a cop." Marcee heaved an exaggerated sigh.

His lips quirked up in a grin.

"What else?" she pressed.

"I don't have time for a relationship." His tone turned serious and his voice filled with regret. "You're something special. You deserve more than a one night stand."

Marcee's heart swelled, moved by the heartfelt sentiment. This man genuinely liked her. Not her pretty face or sexy body, but *her*. Enough that he was willing to walk away from a night of hot sex because he didn't want to hurt her.

Marcee prided herself on her forthrightness. Whenever possible, she liked to be honest. She wished she could tell Sam she liked him. Tell him that from the moment she'd laid eyes on him, she'd felt as if there could be more than just a one night stand between them. Tell him that she'd never met a man with whom she'd so fully connected.

But being smart and savvy in the ways of men, she knew that all honesty would get her would be a night alone in the king-sized bed. If she didn't make Sam believe a casual liaison was okay with her, he'd walk out the door.

"I do deserve more than just one night of any man's attention." She met his gaze head on. "But like you, I don't have time for anything more."

His eyes searched hers, and whatever he found must have reassured him because he took her hand and his thumb caressed her palm. He gave an embarrassed laugh. "I'm also a little rusty at all this."

Shivers of desire traveled up her arm at his touch. If this was out-of-practice, she'd hate to see what he'd be like at full speed.

"And," Sam cleared his throat, "I'm not prepared."

When his gaze met hers, she knew what he was asking. "I have condoms in my purse."

"You do?" Surprise filled his voice.

Marcee lifted her chin. "As far as I'm concerned, safe sex is everyone's responsibility."

"I agree," Sam said, flashing a smile.

A warmth that had nothing to do with room temperature enveloped her. She really liked this guy.

Marcee tugged on the sleeve of his suit jacket.

"Take this off and make yourself comfortable. I'll get more wine."

She rose to her feet and fought to control her nerves. By the way her stomach was flip-flopping, it seemed she'd never done this before.

You haven't, a little voice inside her head whispered, *not with Sam.*

Marcee moved to the cabinet by the bed, splashing some more of Napa Valley's finest into the crystal glasses. But once she finished pouring, she stood staring at the burgundy colored liquid, confused by her tangled emotions.

This is just another one night stand, she told herself firmly. *Nothing more.*

Out of the corner of her eye she saw Sam take off his suit coat and cross the room to stand behind her.

"Second thoughts?" he asked, slipping his arms around her waist.

Marcee closed her eyes and breathed in the clean fresh scent of his shampoo mingled with the spicy tang of his aftershave. He'd held her on the dance floor, but somehow this was different, more intimate.

"We don't have to make love," he whispered against her hair, lightly massaging her shoulders. "We can just talk."

Talk? Was he kidding? She wanted him with an intensity she hadn't even known she was capable of feeling. Just being so close made her body ache with longing. When she turned to face him and saw the desire flickering in his eyes, she smiled, confident that talking wasn't what he wanted, either.

She trailed a perfectly manicured fingernail up his arm. "Talk is highly overrated."

He returned her smile and tugged her toward him. Marcee stared into his eyes and exhaled a ragged breath. She wanted this man in a way that defied logic.

Kiss me. She wasn't sure if she'd said the words or only thought them, but suddenly her arms were around his neck, his around her waist. Her fingers wove through the soft texture of his hair as his mouth obligingly closed over hers.

His lips lingered, drawing her into a whirling spiral of emotions and sensations that seemed profoundly different. There was chemistry between them, an intimacy and spark that she'd never experienced before.

Marcee splayed her hands across his back, feeling the muscles tighten beneath the fabric. She explored his body with a kind of wonder, as if it were the first time she'd ever touched a man. It was new, this desire to linger. To sip instead of gulp. To glide instead of race. When his hands touched her through the soft chiffon, her skin quivered and warmed.

The shadows in the room deepened and the table lamps bathed them in a golden glow, creating a private world just made for two.

"You're gorgeous." Had she said that or had he? Did it matter?

Sam explored the soft skin behind her ears and down her neck, his mouth open against her skin. Everywhere his lips touched she sizzled. She pressed herself against him, lifting her face to his, cursing the fabric that still separated them.

His mouth once again closed over hers, and this time the kiss turned wild, a lush, open-mouthed mating of lips and tongues. When she came up for air, they were both naked.

Marcee drew back and looked her fill. He had a workingman's body—corded with muscle, lean and tan. Dark hair converged on the flat planes of his stomach into a line that disappeared into the waistband of his shorts.

A curious humming filled her body.

"I wondered what you looked like," he said with something akin to awe in his voice.

"You've seen women before," she said softly.

"Not you."

She took a step forward, running her hands over his biceps then trailing them over his chest. "So strong, so—"

"Soft," he said, cupping her large breasts in his palms, his fingers brushing the tips. Her nipples puckered and tingled as he continued his exploration, skimming his hands over intimate dips and hollows.

His touch was gentle and caring. He asked rather than demanded, and she responded fully, without reservation. Her passion, her need for him, grew with each kiss, with each tender caress. By the time Sam retrieved the condoms from her bag and returned to the bed, she was ready for him, every nerve ending on high alert.

He entered her slowly, pushing in a little then retreating, as if making sure she was ready for him. He was big and thick, stretching her. She wrapped her arms around him, pulling him against her, reveling in the long forgotten wonder of being filled by a man intent on pleasing them both.

They moved in perfect rhythm in an age-old ritual that somehow seemed new. She loved the way he felt inside her, rubbing her intimately, filling her. She loved the way his hard body felt over hers. She loved the way his body trembled with pent-up emotion and need as he waited . . . for her.

Her pleasure mounted with each thrust. She closed around him, arched to him. It felt so good, so right. She couldn't remember the last time she'd been so happy. She celebrated her happiness noisily, determined to wring every last drop of pleasure from the moment.

Marcee rode the building pressure until their bodies were damp and sweaty, and still she clung to him. And when the combination of emotion and physical sensation sent her crashing over the edge, it seemed right that she was in his arms when the world exploded.

3

"*He's Fern's father?*" Shock made Marcee's voice extra loud, and a couple of women across the room in the downtown Chicago coffee shop turned to stare.

"Yes, he is." Fresh back from a honeymoon in Fiji, Jenny wore her happiness on her sleeve. Marcee had the feeling her friend would have kept smiling even if she'd said the place was on fire.

"How was I supposed to know?" Marcee knew she should have made the connection. But the minute she'd seen the man, all rational thought fled her brain. "He never said his daughter's name was Fern."

"His last name is McKelvey," Jenny pointed out. "How much clearer could it be?"

And Fern had said her father was there, a tiny voice inside Marcee's head reminded her. But she'd never paid attention to Fern's last name or the fact that her father had been somewhere in the large ballroom. There was no reason.

"You're sure he's her *father*?" The word felt awkward on her tongue.

"Positive." Jenny brought a piece of biscotti to her lips, her large diamond glittering in the light. "There was only one Sam McKelvey on the guest list."

Marcee shook her head. "I can't believe I spent the night with Fern's dad."

She couldn't figure out why the thought was so disconcerting. Maybe it was because she knew Fern. Or maybe it was that Sam seemed too hunky to be anyone's dad.

"It's not like he's some archetypical father figure." Jenny's lips quirked upward. "He's young. And incredibly hot."

"You're right," Marcee said, nodding. "And it was just a one time, er, one night thing."

"It doesn't have to be—a one night thing, I mean." Jenny peered at Marcee over the rim of her cup. "You *could* call him."

Though Marcee wasn't averse to calling men, she knew she wouldn't be picking up the phone anytime soon. While Sam had given her his number, he hadn't asked for hers. And he'd made it clear—in a very nice way—that he didn't have time for a relationship. "I've been really busy lately."

"Don't wait too long." Jenny motioned the waiter for the check. "I hear he's moving."

Marcee straightened in her chair. "Where?"

"I think he has a new job, but I could be wrong." She put a finger to her lips and thought for a moment. "Robert and I were over at my parents' house for dinner the other night and Annie mentioned something about it."

"What's he going to be doing?" Marcee knew she was showing way too much interest in the man's life, but she couldn't help herself.

"Some kind of police work." Jenny pulled her brows together. "In a small town."

Marcee fought a pang of envy. Though she firmly believed Sam would regret the move, he'd done it. He'd seized the day.

"If you'd like," Jenny said, her voice breaking through Marcee's reverie, "I could get the scoop from my sister,"

Marcee waved a dismissive hand. "Don't bother. I was just curious."

Yes, even though she could remember the heat of his touch without closing her eyes, Sam Mc-Kelvey was history. She'd already relegated his hot kisses and heart-tugging smile to the past. It had been simply a one night stand . . . and she wasn't about to pretend otherwise.

"That's a great color for you." The thin bleached-blond man behind the cosmetics counter narrowed his gaze. "Not many redheads can wear that shade."

Marcee perked up beneath his admiring gaze. After leaving the coffee shop, she'd planned to head straight back to her apartment. But Jenny's news had reminded her of Sam, and she'd felt the need for a little pick-me-up.

"Ma'am?" The clerk's voice brought Marcee back to the present. *Ma'am?* Had this superbly attired metrosexual really called her ma'am?

"We're running a free gift until the end of the month with the purchase of our age-defying night cream," he continued, sounding incredibly perky. "I have a sample I'd like to give you to try for a few nights. I think you'll be amazed at the difference it makes on fine lines and wrinkles."

Fine lines? Wrinkles?

Marcee jerked her gaze to the mirror on the counter, her heart pounding. She stared critically at the reflection. Maybe there were a couple of barely perceptible fine lines on her forehead, but she couldn't locate a single wrinkle anywhere on her face.

She lifted her gaze back to the clerk and found him shifting from one foot to the other, as if trying to decide whether to stay or make a run for it.

"I hope you understand I wasn't implying that *you* had any wrinkles," he said, offering a conciliatory smile. "Your skin is perfect, flawless, *magnifique.* I merely suggested the cream as a preventative measure. Sample it. See—"

"Forget the samples," Marcee said, her gaze darting back to the mirror . . . and her forehead. "Give me the big jar."

She'd barely pulled out her credit card when she heard a squeal and her name. Even before she turned, she had a good idea who she'd find. Dressed alike and looking perfectly adorable in capris, skimpy cotton shirts, and flip-flips, she saw Annie Carman and Fern McKelvey.

Marcee smiled. "What brings you girls downtown?"

"What does it look like?" Annie laughed and both girls held up their bags. "Fern's moving so we decided to go on one last shopping spree courtesy of her dad's credit card."

Her dad. For a moment Marcee let her gaze linger on Fern. She'd watched the girl grow up alongside Annie. But until this moment she'd never paid her much attention.

Now that she'd taken the time to look, Marcee could see the resemblance. Fern had Sam's dark hair and hazel eyes. Their features were similar, though Fern's were of course more feminine. There hadn't been anything feminine about Sam McKelvey . . .

"I thought you were with my sister." Annie glanced around as if expecting Jenny to magically appear.

"I was," Marcee said. "But she had to hurry home. She and Robert were meeting with the architect."

Though Robert had a to-die-for condo close to Navy Pier and overlooking Lake Michigan, he and Jenny had recently purchased some land in the northern suburbs. Marcee hadn't even blinked when her former workaholic friend confided she couldn't wait to fill their new home with the pitter-patter of little feet. Lately, life had been just one surprise after the other.

"Fern's getting a new house," Annie announced. "A big square box of a house with a large front porch and swing."

"It's not really new," Fern clarified. "It's close to eighty years old but in great shape."

The description fit to a tee the kind of house Marcee had grown up in . . . the one she'd been kicked out of . . . the one where her mother and now teenage stepbrother still lived.

"How come you're moving?" Marcee kept her gaze focused on the girls even as she scrawled her name on a credit card receipt.

"My dad got a different job," Fern said. "He wants us to spend more time together."

Annie shot her friend a teasing glance. "Fern's dad is going to be her new best friend."

"No." Fern shook her head and met Annie's gaze. "You'll always be my best friend."

It was sweet, Marcee thought as she took the bag of beauty supplies from the clerk. Touching. A tad schmaltzy. Still, she couldn't help thinking back to her high school friendship with Iris Lang. The two musketeers, everyone had called them. It was funny; she hadn't thought of Iris in years.

"Are you excited about going to a new school?" she asked Fern.

"You bet," Fern said. "With Annie graduating, Barrington won't be the same anyway. And I tend to make friends easily."

Things must have changed dramatically since

she'd been in high school, Marcee decided. At Ellwood High everyone had their friends locked in by seventh grade and most weren't interested in adding anyone new to the group. Of course, her school had been small and very cliquish.

"Where is it you're moving?" she asked.

"Ohmygod, that's Jason Hinke," Annie said in an under-the-breath squeal, her blue eyes snapping with excitement.

"And he's with Kyle Radcliffe," Fern said in a just as excited whisper.

"We gotta go." Annie grabbed Fern's arm and then met Marcee's gaze with a lopsided grin. "Seize the moment and all that . . . you understand."

Marcee flashed a smile. If anyone understood such behavior, she did. After all, her life was one carpe diem after the other.

Sam gazed over the top of the newspaper at his daughter, shocked to find her up at this hour. Usually he ate breakfast alone. But when he walked into the kitchen, there was a bowl of cereal and a frosty glass of orange juice on the table for him.

He wasn't sure what surprised him most . . . that Fern had breakfast waiting or that she had rolled out of bed so early. Of course 7:00 A.M. wasn't *that* early, considering that she'd spent last night watching a movie with him instead of being out late with friends.

While part of him was pleased—after all, spending quality time with her *was* the primary reason he'd taken the position in Ellwood—another part wished she'd made some new friends. "So, what's on the agenda for today?"

"Camden and I are going to Two Rivers," Fern said. "But that won't be until noon. He's not into early."

Sam's fingers tightened around the juice glass. Camden Smith seemed polite enough the few times he'd met the boy, but he still had his reservations. Camden was so different from the other boys his daughter had dated back in the city. The truth was, he had no idea what his bright, beautiful, talented daughter saw in the skinny redhead. "The guys at the station say Camden is bad news," he said, and sensed as much as saw Fern react.

She lowered her glass of juice to the table and lifted a perfectly arched brow.

"Ron and Dick?" his daughter said, her tone making it clear what she thought of his deputies. "The same two who think rock music comes straight from radio station DEVIL?"

"Point taken," Sam said with a rueful smile.

"I never thought I'd hear you quote those guys." Fern scooped up the last *O* in her bowl with her spoon. "You'd better be careful or you're going to end up being a closed-minded jerk, just like them."

"They're not all bad," Sam said, feeling the need to defend his deputies. "But I admit they do tend to see things as black or white."

"I don't know what they've got against Cam," Fern said. "He's never been in any kind of trouble."

Sam knew that was true, because if the boy *had* been cited for any reason, he would have heard about it. In the month he'd been in Ellwood, he'd been brought up to speed on the history of almost every resident in the community.

Though he refused to bad-mouth his deputies to Fern, their attitude did trouble him. Ron and Dick tended to label anything that followed Ellwood norms as "good." Everything else was "bad."

"It's probably the fact that he refused to go out for basketball last year," Sam said.

At six-two, Camden would have been a welcome addition to the height-challenged roster of the Ellwood Tigers. But according to Ron, the boy had refused to give it a try.

"Practice would have interfered with Youth Symphony rehearsals," Fern said.

"Youth symphony?" Sam paused. "Ellwood doesn't have a youth symphony."

"Chicago does."

Sam knew all about the Chicago Youth Symphony from a former coworker whose daughter had played oboe in the select orchestra. "CYSO is extremely competitive."

"Cam is very talented." Fern lifted her chin. "You'd realize that if you spent more time talking to him rather than judging him."

Sam wanted to trust her instincts, but he was a father and he didn't want her tied down to *any* boy at her age. "All I'm saying is that there are lots of nice boys in town and I don't want to see you get so serious—"

"I'm not 'so serious.'" Fern's voice rose and her hazel eyes—so like his own—snapped. "He's my *friend*. Why can't you just be glad I have a friend here?"

"It's not that—"

"Nothing I ever do is right." Fern stood and shoved back her chair with a clatter.

He caught a glimpse of hot anger in her eyes before she turned and stormed from the room. An increasingly familiar knot took up residence in the pit of his stomach. Spending so much time with Fern had been both a blessing and a curse. He'd definitely enjoyed getting to know her better, but had never realized how moody teenage girls could be.

Like now. They'd been having what he considered a perfectly rational discussion when she'd snapped. Gone berserk just because he suggested she expand her group of friends.

Sam leaned back in his chair and wiped a hand across his face. It was times like these when he worried that moving to Ellwood had been a mistake. They'd both discovered that making new friends in a close-knit community wasn't as easy as one might think.

Oh, people were friendly. But they often had their own agenda. And he had to constantly remember that even the most innocent of actions could be misconstrued. Like last week when he'd shared a casual lunch with one of the female dispatchers. By the time he went home, the town had them practically walking down the aisle.

He'd realized then that if he hoped to get a good reference at the end of his contract, he had to be a model citizen, on and off duty. Thankfully, so far there hadn't been any distractions . . . or temptations. Not a Marcee Robbens in sight.

The night he'd spent with the beautiful redhead hadn't been nearly long enough. She was bold and funny, and when he was with her, he'd felt incredibly alive.

Even after all these months, he still thought about calling her. He didn't have her number but knew it wouldn't be hard to get. Every time he'd picked up the phone to call Jenny, however, he put the receiver down without dialing a single number.

No, for the next year Fern and his job had to be his priority. There was no room in his life for a green-eyed redhead who'd made him feel alive again. No room at all.

The sign at the road's edge said ELLWOOD,
ILLINOIS. The knot in Marcee's stomach said coming home was a big mistake. When she'd left her
hometown as a teenager, she vowed never to return. Now here she was, coming back with her
tail between her legs.

No, she corrected herself. She'd chosen to come
back. Taking care of her brother was the right
thing to do.

Still, with each passing mile she'd begun to realize that doing the right thing wasn't always as
easy as it sounded. As the Jetta crossed into the
city limits, Marcee tightened her fingers around

the steering wheel and forced herself to breathe.

The town had grown since she'd lived here. According to the sign, the bedroom community fifty miles north of Chicago had over 2,500 residents. With its well-kept Victorian homes, picturesque town square, and a plethora of new housing developments, she could see why young professionals found the place appealing.

For those desiring both small town life and big city salaries, Ellwood offered affordable housing and an easy commute. Despite the many advantages, however, she had never been the slightest bit tempted to return. Yet somehow she'd agreed to live here for an entire year.

Was she crazy?

Ahead on the right she saw a sign advertising the Grateful Bread Bakery and Café. The business had been *the* place to go when she was in high school. Back then the bakery was known simply as "Lang's" and their whole wheat sourdough cinnamon rolls were famous throughout the region. Ernest and Twyla Lang had built a loyal clientele around such favorites.

The older couple had tried hard to interest their only child, DeLynn, in the business. Unfortunately, the young blonde had been more interested in smoking pot and following the Grateful Dead than in baking bread with her parents.

When Ernest and Twyla were killed in an accident on I-94 several years ago, it hadn't been a surprise that the bakery was willed to their granddaughter, Iris.

The girl had been born after one of DeLynn's many trips to the West Coast. As soon as the new mother could travel, she'd been back on the road, leaving behind her newborn baby for her parents to rear.

Growing up, Iris Lang had been Marcee's best friend. Like her, Iris always stood just outside the Ellwood mainstream. Not because of her café-au-lait skin or her honey-colored Afro, but because, like Marcee, the beautiful and intelligent Iris *chose* to be there. She was an independent spirit who had little tolerance for the game playing that permeated small town society.

After high school Marcee had lost touch with Iris, but she'd heard her old friend was back in town. Having lived in California for a number of years, Iris had returned to take over the bakery after her grandparents' death.

Impulsively, Marcee wheeled the Jetta into the deserted parking lot. It was just after ten, late enough that she'd missed the morning rush hour and was too early for the lunch surge. Though Tom wanted her at the house as early as possible, as far as Marcee was concerned, there was always time for an espresso and a scone.

She pulled into a stall just left of the front door. Through the large plate-glass window she glimpsed a woman with hair the color of burnt caramel bent over the bakery case.

A sudden chill swept over Marcee. What if it *was* true? What if you really couldn't go home again? What if she'd been fooling herself?

She shifted her gaze back the way she'd just come, tempted to put the car in reverse and forget all about trying to be good.

Then she caught sight of the lime green band around her right wrist, the soft rubber imprinted with the words REACH HIGH. It had been there for over a month, reminding her each time she wavered, each time she was tempted to quit, that change, any change, started with a single step.

Marcee closed her eyes briefly and took a deep breath. She might be many things, but she'd never been a coward. With that thought in mind, she unbuckled her seat belt, pulled the keys from the ignition, and stepped out of the car.

A melodious jingling of bells heralded her entry

into the bakery. She'd barely passed through the doorway when the tantalizing aroma of freshly made cinnamon rolls teased her nostrils. She took a deep breath and stood there for a second, reveling in all the delicious smells.

Behind the bakery case, the proprietor straightened. "May I help—" Shock danced across Iris Lang's face. Her brilliant blue eyes widened and she gave a little squeal. "Marcee Robbens? Is that really you?"

Marcee smiled broadly, her heart warmed by the welcome in her friend's voice. "Hello, Iris. It's been a long time."

The words hadn't even left her lips when Iris rounded the bakery case.

Iris gave her a big hug. "I'm so happy to see you," she said, and took a step back, holding Marcee at arm's length. "You're sure lookin' good."

"You look pretty fabulous yourself," Marcee said, letting her gaze linger on the trim and stylish Iris.

From the cropped jeans that accentuated her long legs to the jade-colored cotton top that made her skin look like warm honey, Iris oozed style. The large dangling earrings might be vintage Iris, but the chin-length razor cut hair was new.

"The gossips said you were coming back, but

I told 'em I had to see you before I'd believe it," Iris said.

Marcee laughed. "So much for slipping into town unnoticed."

"You know that's impossible, in this town, anyway." Iris chuckled. "How about I buy you a cup of coffee? You and me, we've got some catching up to do."

Marcee fingered her lime green bracelet. She might be able to deflect the more general questions of the Ellwood citizenry, but Iris would not be so easily appeased. No, if she stayed for coffee, she'd have no choice but to come clean. Still, if anyone would understand, it would be Iris.

Glancing at the bakery case, Marcee smiled. "Make it an espresso and throw in a peach scone and you've got a deal."

Ten minutes later the two old friends sat at a table by the window, a plate of scones and two cups of espresso before them.

"I heard your mother has got herself a new man." Iris broke off a piece of scone and popped it into her mouth.

Marcee took a sip of espresso, relishing the strong, bitter taste on her tongue. She chose her words carefully, not because she feared Iris would repeat her confidences, but because she'd promised herself that she wouldn't gossip. But simply relaying facts wasn't gossiping.

"From what my brother told me, Shirleen met hubby number five at a biker rally in Sturgis." Calling her mom by her given name was awkward, but Marcee refused to call the woman who'd disappointed her so many times "Mother."

Iris nodded. "I heard that."

"Then you probably also know that Mad Dog— I don't remember his real name—is an over-the-road truck driver." Marcee pulled her brows together trying to remember what else Tom had told her. "When he asked Shirleen to go with him, apparently she jumped at the chance. In the excitement, she must have forgotten that her youngest son still had another year of high school."

Though Marcee was trying hard to be factual, the last sentence came out with a liberal dose of sarcasm. Realizing she was dangerously close to bad-mouthing her mother, she pressed her lips tightly together until the urge to say more passed.

Iris shook her head. "Some women should never be mothers."

Marcee dipped her head in a slight nod, again stifling the urge to add her two cents. Gossip was on her list of behaviors to avoid, as was bad-mouthing someone. Agreeing with something that was the truth probably didn't fall into either category, but she wasn't taking any chances.

"Is Tom excited to be moving to Seattle?" Iris asked when the silence lengthened.

"Seems to be." Marcee's half brother—from her mother's second marriage—was an environmental engineer who'd always dreamed of working in the Pacific Northwest. "When he called, his new job was all he could talk about . . . that and what to do about Camden."

"I'm happy for Tom," Iris said slowly. "But I still can't figure out why Cam isn't going with them. After all, Shirleen made it clear she wasn't coming back."

Marcee hesitated. She refused to lie to Iris, but neither would she break Tom's confidence. Tom had told her that his wife, Celia, threw a fit when he suggested bringing Cam with them to Seattle. But thankfully it hadn't become an issue because the next morning Camden had told Tom—in no uncertain terms—to not bother asking him to come along, because he was staying put.

"Tom said Camden wanted to stay in Ellwood," Marcee said simply. "Finish his senior year."

"That surprises me." Iris broke off another piece of scone. "Cam comes in sometimes after school.

He's cool, which means he no more fits in here than you and I did. I can't believe he wants to stay."

Marcee took her time chewing. What could she say? She wouldn't know Camden Smith, her half brother from her mother's third marriage, if he walked through the door. He'd just turned three when she was kicked out of the house, and she hadn't been home since.

"What about you?" Iris asked. "How were you able to swing coming here on such short notice? Is your job setting you up to work from home?"

The same sick feeling that had filled Marcee's stomach when she'd been walked out of the large accounting firm's corporate offices that fateful Monday returned. She shifted her gaze to the bakery shop door, willing someone to walk through it.

"If you're looking for the cavalry, the lunch crowd won't arrive until after eleven," Iris said.

Marcee jerked her gaze to find Iris staring, a knowing smile on her lips.

"If you don't want to discuss your job, I'm cool with that," Iris said. "We can chat about anything you want. You know me, I just like to talk."

Marcee couldn't help but smile. She remembered well their all-night gab sessions in high school. She and Iris would spend hours discussing boys and clothes and school. Then, once those topics were exhausted, they'd switch gears and fantasize about how much better their lives would be once they left Ellwood. How idealistic they'd both been . . .

Marcee glanced at the woman across the table. While she may not have seen Iris in fourteen years, she knew that whatever she told her wouldn't go any further.

"I don't work at D and D anymore." Marcee lifted her chin. "I was fired."

Iris gasped. "No way."

Marcee resisted the urge to sigh. "Way."

Being let go had been a blow. Though she hadn't loved her job, she'd liked it, along with most of the people who worked there.

Iris's brows pulled together in puzzlement. "But you'd been there forever. I know firms are scaling back but why would they let you go?"

Marcee met her friend's gaze. "I refused to sleep with a client."

"Whoa. Say what?" Iris sputtered. "They can't fire you for that."

"The whole situation was, shall we say, complicated." Marcee fought to keep her tone matter-of-fact even as anger surged. Though she'd kept her cool through the whole messy ordeal, the injustice of it all still rankled.

"How complicated?" Iris asked.

Marcee took a sip of coffee, using the time to pull her thoughts together. "This guy, Harry, had been in Chicago meeting with my boss, Rich Dodson. I went with some friends to a hotel bar after work. Harry was there and recognized me from D and D."

Iris leaned forward and rested her elbows on the table, giving Marcee her full attention.

Marcee took a breath and continued. "He seemed nice enough, . . . until I refused to sleep with him."

The crazy thing was, if it had been a month earlier, she probably would have gone up to his hotel room with him. But after Sam . . . well, she just couldn't do it. She'd told herself it was because she'd had the best and wouldn't settle for less. But there was more to it than that.

"I take it he didn't like being told no," Iris said.

"He came unglued. Did a Jekyll and Hyde." Marcee shivered, remembering the dangerous glint in Harry's eyes. "The last words he said to me, or rather *yelled*, when I walked away was that I'd be sorry."

"Then what happened?" Iris spoke in a hushed

tone, though she and Marcee were the only ones in the bakery.

"Nothing. Until I showed up for work Monday. That's when I discovered that Harry had made good on his promise. He'd registered a formal complaint. Told my boss *I'd* been all over him. Said he'd been appalled by my "unprofessional" behavior. Gave Rich an ultimatum: fire me or he was walking and taking his business with him."

"Bastard," Iris spat the word, her perfectly tweezed brows pulled together like two thunderclouds.

"That wasn't the worst of it." After the incident, she'd been so embarrassed that she hadn't told anyone the part that really hurt. But with Iris looking at her, with those large blue eyes filled with understanding, she found herself wanting to get it all off her chest. "My boss believed I was trying to sleep with the guy to ensure he did business with the firm."

"No—"

"Yes," Marcee said. "Rich looked me right in the eye and told me that while he couldn't keep me on—the account was too large to risk losing—he admired my initiative."

Normally never at a loss for words, Marcee

had been struck dumb when what he was saying sank in. For ten years she'd prided herself on being a top notch CPA, a "go to" person for her colleagues. A professional.

But when Rich Dodson congratulated her for trying to help the company, she'd realized she was a joke. A piece of fluff. And worse yet, she had no one to blame but herself. She'd played it free and easy for too many years.

When she'd left home at seventeen, she was determined to make something of herself. To rise above her stepfather's expectations. To show everyone that she was more than a pretty face and big boobs. But somewhere along the way she'd failed.

She exhaled a heavy sigh and looked up to find Iris gazing at her, her eyes filled with sympathy.

"I'm so sorry that happened to you." Iris reached over and gave her hand a squeeze. "But I'm glad you're here."

"When Tom called I was trying to decide whether to sign another year's lease on my apartment."

Making the decision to return to Ellwood hadn't been an easy one. But there was nothing tying her to Chicago, and the truth was, her heart had gone out to Cam. Though she didn't know the boy, she knew what it felt like to be seventeen, unwanted and alone in the world.

When Tom had confided that Celia thought the kid was a "loser," tears had stung her eyes. She wasn't sure if they were for Cam or for herself. It was what her stepfather always called her.

Maybe he was right.

No. She gave the thought a swift kick into the stratosphere. Marcee Robbens might be down but she wasn't out.

"It almost seems as if you were meant to return to Ellwood," Iris said.

"That's how it seemed to me, too." Caring for Camden would be a new start for her; a chance to prove that she was capable of thinking of someone other than herself. And it would give her time to figure out what she wanted to do with the rest of her life.

"That's an interesting bracelet." Iris's gaze lingered on Marcee's right wrist. "Reminds me of the Lance Armstrong one."

Marcee shifted her gaze to the lime green band with REACH HIGH imprinted in the soft rubber. She couldn't help but smile.

"I got it at one of those empowerment seminars for women. It serves as a reminder of all I can accomplish." The enthusiasm she'd felt when she sat in that vast arena surrounded by thousands of other women returned and spilled over into her voice. "I'd been feeling down ever since this guy I met at a wedding didn't want to see me again. Then the whole fiasco at D and D happened—"

"You've lost me," Iris said. "What does any of that have to do with the bracelet? Or the seminar?"

"I decided it was time to make some changes," Marcee said.

"Still not making the connection."

Marcee realized she needed to start at the beginning. "When I got kicked out of the house at seventeen," she said, "I always thought I'd handled the situation pretty well. I finished high school. Got some grants. Went to college, then started at D and D."

Iris nodded her head approvingly.

"It was only at the seminar, listening to the stories, that I realized I hadn't come through unscathed." Marcee took a deep breath. "All these years, I've settled for less because deep down I didn't feel like I deserved more. The seminar leaders helped me realize that if I keep doing what I've always done, I'm going to get what I've always gotten. That's not what I want. I don't want to sleep with men who won't remember my name the next morning. Or work for an employer who thinks I'd prostitute myself for the company. I want to be respected. To be the type of woman *I* can respect."

By the time she finished, she was out of breath and Iris's eyes had taken on a glazed look.

"Good for you," Iris said, blinked and shook herself as if coming out of a stupor. "Any idea how you're going to accomplish this metamorphosis?"

"I'm going to demand more, from myself and from others." Marcee thought back to the night with Sam. The time she'd spent with him had changed her, had changed how she viewed making love. "No more settling."

"You'll do it. You've always been able to do anything you set your mind to do," Iris said. "Remember when you wanted to develop that system in high school to score the way a guy kissed? Everyone said it couldn't be done."

"Seventy-three percent of the girls in grades nine through twelve participated." A smile of satisfaction lifted Marcee's lips. Not only had the project been the talk of the school, working those figures had spurred her interest in math. "I still can see Ron Densmore's face when he saw the results. I think if I'd been a guy, he would have punched me out."

Ron had been at the bottom of the list, and once the report got out, was the recipient of a lot of teasing, not all of it good-natured. When he confronted her, she was less than sympathetic. She'd told him it was his fault since no girl liked wet, slobbery kisses.

"Ron is now a deputy sheriff," Iris said, as if she'd read Marcee's mind.

"Tom warned me," Marcee said. "Told me I'd better make sure I don't speed or double park."

Iris's eyes took on an assessing gleam. "He's still single. Just broke up with his girlfriend."

Even after all these years Marcee recognized that look. She groaned. "Tell me you're not still into playing matchmaker."

"Okay, cross Ron off the list," Iris said. "I can see where your past interactions with the man might make it hard to date him."

"I'm not looking to date anybody, remember?" She lowered her voice. "Besides, I hate wet, slobbery kisses."

Ignoring that last comment, Iris tapped her index finger against the table. "What about our new sheriff? I don't know him all that well but he's single and a real hunk. I think the two of you would hit it off."

God save me from well-meaning friends.

"Not interested." Marcee leaned back in her seat. "Anyway, if this guy is so hot, why don't you go for him?"

"I like my men a little more brown, if you know what I mean," Iris said with a wink. She shifted her gaze out the front window and her face brightened. "Speak of the devil."

Marcee pulled her brows together. "What devil?"

"The handsome one in my parking lot." Iris pushed back her chair and stood. "Our new sheriff is headed toward the front door. I know you've never put much stock in my matchmaking skill, but trust me. When you see this guy, the first words out of your mouth are going to be 'Iris, you were right.'"

Marcee rolled her eyes. Her friend always had a flare for the dramatic.

The bells over the door jingled and Marcee shifted in her seat to face the door. But when the man stepped into the bakery and she caught sight of his face, her polite smile vanished.

A roaring filled her ears.

Her heart stopped beating.

"Iris," she breathed. "You were right."

When Sam had been shot in the chest several years before, his Kevlar vest protected him, but the impact knocked the air out of his lungs. He remembered the feeling. He felt the same way now.

Dressed in olive green shorts that made her legs look like they went on forever, and a V-necked yellow shirt that showed an obscene amount of cleavage, sat the woman who'd been haunting his dreams.

As their eyes met, her mouth formed a perfect O, and Sam realized he wasn't the only one surprised.

"What are you doing in Ellwood?" she stammered.

Iris shifted a curious gaze from Sam to Marcee, then back to Sam. "You two know each other?"

Sam smiled. "It's good to see you again, Marcee."

"Hello, Sam."

The low husky voice reminded him of tangled bed sheets and sweat-slicked skin. His body stirred but he did his best to shut it down. None of this was making sense. Especially the impersonal smile on her lips.

Marcee shifted her gaze to Iris. "I've known Sam's daughter, Fern, since she was a little girl. Fern is best friends with the sister of a friend of mine."

Marcee knew *Fern*? It took everything in Sam to hide his surprise. He'd never considered the possibility. But he realized now he should have known. After all, Annie Carman and Fern were friends for years, and the Carman house had been Fern's second home. With Marcee being best friends with Jenny Carman, it only figured that she would know his daughter.

"O-kay," Iris said, her brows pulled together in confusion. "I think I understand the connection."

"Marcee and I recently met for the first time at a wedding," Sam said, strolling over to the front of the café where the two women sat by the window. The sultry scent of Marcee's perfume teased his nostrils and brought back vivid memories of her and him, in that king-sized bed with limbs entwined. And not only did she *smell* good, she looked fabulous. Her hair framed her face in loose waves, drawing attention to her emerald eyes.

But he was a man, after all, and his gaze couldn't help but drop lower to appreciate how well her shirt emphasized the size of her breasts. His mouth went dry.

He told himself to lift his gaze, admire the curve of her neckline. The creaminess of her skin. The vibrant green of her eyes.

Instead he mentally stripped away her shirt, envisioning the scrap of lace beneath. A scrap of lace he'd dispose of with a flick of his fingers . . .

"I'd heard that Sam and Fern moved to a small town . . . "

Marcee gave a little laugh, and when he looked up, her face was flushed, her eyes glittery, as if she'd been sharing his fantasy.

" . . . I just had no idea it was to my home town."

The puzzle pieces locked into place. She'd told him she grew up in a small town. He just hadn't realized it was *this* one.

That meant she hadn't come to see him. Sam

shoved aside a twinge of disappointment. It was ridiculous thinking for even one second that she'd have tracked him down.

"Sam, how about I get you a cup of coffee and one of those coconut muffins you like so much?" Iris said. "That way you can sit and relax while you catch up with Marcee."

Sam cast a questioning glance at Marcee. "As long as I'm not intrud—"

"Don't be silly." Iris grabbed his arm, pulled out a chair and shoved him into it. "Sit. I'll be right back."

The minute Iris left, Sam reached over and took Marcee's hand, her skin warm beneath his. "It's so good to see you."

Marcee gently pulled her hand back, offering him the kind of smile you'd give a distant relative. "How's Fern?"

Her voice still had that sultry edge, but her words were merely polite. If he didn't have such vivid memories of the taste and feel of her, he would have been tempted to believe his daughter was their only connection.

Sam pushed down a rising frustration. Now that they were alone—or as alone as one could be with Iris twenty feet away—he thought she'd loosen up. Smile that "come hither" smile that stirred his blood, say something boldly suggestive. Instead she wanted to talk about . . . Fern?

"She's fine," Sam said. "Acclimating as best she can to small town life."

"It's not easy."

Sam heaved a heavy sigh. "No, it's not."

For the first time since he'd seen her, a sparkle lit Marcee's eyes. "I don't like to say it, but I told you so."

Sam couldn't help but grin. "Yes, you did."

His gaze met hers, and though she made no move to touch him, the essence of her surrounded him, holding him immobile. Suddenly he was back in the hotel room, laughing and talking with her and feeling that connection.

It was the strength of that bond that had kept him from calling her. Though it had been years since he was involved in a relationship, he'd watched the guys he worked with enough to know the score. Relationships, especially new ones, tended to be all-consuming.

Fern had come in second to his career since she'd been born, and this was his last shot. One more chance to forge a relationship with his only child so she could go out into the world knowing she wasn't alone, that her dad was on her side.

If only I'd met Marcee later . . .

"Sam," Marcee said in a low tone. "I need a favor."

"Anything," he said without even needing to think.

"I don't want anyone to know we were personally involved."

It was a simple request. Perfectly understandable, considering the nature of small towns. Why, then, did he feel as if he'd just been slapped down?

Marcee cast a sideways glance as if to make sure Iris wasn't anywhere near before continuing. "Coming back here is a way for me to start over. A one night stand isn't who I am anymore."

Now he was confused. "We didn't have a one night stand."

"Yes, we did."

"No, we didn't."

"What else would you call it?" Marcee lowered her voice to a whisper. "We met, got together one time, and that was it," she said tersely.

"A one night stand is just about sex," he said. "That wasn't the way it was—"

"I'm not going to argue semantics with you," she said. "Just keep quiet, okay?"

Even if she hadn't asked, he wasn't the kind of guy to kiss and tell. But he knew that acting as if they barely knew each other would be hard for him to do.

"Sam, please." Two tiny lines of worry furrowed her brow. "For me."

When she put it that way, how could he refuse? "I'll—"

"Here you go." Iris set a muffin and coffee before him, then pulled out a chair and sat down. She smiled brightly and shifted her gaze to Marcee. "So you two met at a wedding?"

Sam didn't want to think of weddings. They made him think of Marcee. Marcee, who'd decided she wanted nothing to do with him. He forked off a piece of muffin with extra force. How was he going to pretend she meant nothing to him when he couldn't keep his eyes off her? "Torture."

"Torture?" Iris brought a hand to her chest in a melodramatic gesture. "What makes you say that?"

Sam stifled a groan, realizing he'd spoken aloud. He cast a sideways glance at Marcee, who sat eating her scone, now looking bored with the conversation. His frustration mounted.

"Suit and tie required," Sam said. "Boring ceremony followed by equally boring reception."

Iris laughed, but Marcee looked disappointed.

"C'mon, Sheriff," Iris teased. "I bet you've met your share of beautiful women at weddings."

Her tone and manner was playful, encouraging confidences. Sam couldn't believe the change in her. He'd been in her shop a half-dozen times and she'd never been so talkative.

"I think most men have," he admitted, resisting the urge to look at Marcee. "In fact my deputy, Ron, met his former girlfriend at a wedding."

"I bet you didn't know Deputy Ron went to school with Marcee and me," Iris said.

Sam shifted his gaze to Marcee. "I didn't know you and Ron were friends."

"Friends." Iris chuckled as if Sam had said something funny. "Hardly."

Sam ignored her and focused on Marcee. "You went to school together . . . "

"We did," Marcee said. "But Ron and I were never friends."

She didn't say it, but Sam got the distinct impression she didn't care much for his deputy.

"Marcee is sugar-coating," Iris said. "Not only wasn't Ron her friend, the guy hated her. One time he was so angry he almost hit her."

A protective urge rose up inside Sam, surprising him with its intensity. He didn't like the idea of anyone hating Marcee. He clenched his jaw. And by God, nobody better hurt her, either.

"Don't be so dramatic, Iris." Marcee shot her friend an annoyed look. "High school was a long time ago."

"If Ron, or anyone, ever bothers you," Sam said, his voice tight with control, "you come to me. Understand?"

"He probably doesn't even remember me," Marcee said.

He pinned her with his gaze. "Promise me."

"Ohh, I do so love a forceful man," Iris gushed. "Don't you, Marcee?"

"Shut up, Iris," Marcee said, her tone saccharine sweet.

"Marcee?" Sam said, wanting her assurance.

"I promise," she said.

"Now that we've got that settled," Iris smiled brightly, "what shall we talk about?"

Sam kept his gaze focused on Marcee. "What brings you back to Ellwood?"

She traced the rim of her cup with the tip of her finger. "I'm going to be taking care of my kid brother for the next year."

Sam pulled his gaze away, remembering all too well how that finger felt traveling up the hard length of him. "That's wonderful," he finally managed to spit out. "Are you going to work remote?"

"I'm not at D and D anymore," she said in a matter-of-fact tone. "But my severance package will more than tide me over."

He found himself curious about the severance deal, but it wasn't his business. "Good for you," he said, remembering her talk about being in a rut and wanting to get out. "When did—"

The ring of his phone stopped him cold. Seeing Marcee had made him forget everything, even the fact that he was on duty. Sam pulled the cell from his pocket and flipped it open. "McKelvey."

He listened to the dispatcher relay information about a fender bender. "I'm on my way." He snapped the phone shut and met their curious stares. "Noninjury accident on Old Farm Road, out by the highway."

Iris rose to her feet. "I'll get you a to-go cup."

Sam knew he should be out the door and headed to his cruiser, but he couldn't make himself leave. His gaze lingered on Marcee. "I'll be seeing you."

It wasn't so much a question as a promise.

"I imagine you will," she said with a slight smile. "The town isn't all that big."

"I'd better go."

"Tell Fern hello."

"I will."

"Here's your coffee." Iris held out a cup, and Sam rose to his feet.

He took the cup from Iris and pressed a couple bills into her hand. "Thanks."

Though he didn't look back, he swore he could feel Marcee's eyes on him all the way to the cruiser.

The door had barely shut when Iris turned to Marcee. "Sam McKelvey was the guy from the wedding," she said triumphantly. "The one who dissed you."

The second the comment had left Sam's mouth, Marcee knew Iris was too smart, too savvy, not to make the connection.

Maybe it would be good if Iris knew the whole story.

She didn't give the ridiculous thought any consideration. It was going to be hard enough having Sam in the same town without having anyone— including Iris—know their history.

"He is." Marcee tried to keep her tone light. "Sam and I met at my friend Jenny's wedding. We danced, had some champagne, talked. Generally just had a nice time. But at the end of the evening he didn't ask for my number. It kind of bummed me out for a while. I'm okay with it now."

So maybe it wasn't the whole truth but at least she hadn't lied.

When an understanding look filled Iris's gaze, Marcee knew she was home free.

"I've had that happen to me, too," she said. "You meet a guy and seem to have this great connection . . . then discover it was all one-sided."

"Yep." Marcee resisted the urge to sigh. "That's pretty much how it played out."

"He is cute," Iris said. "And did you see the look in his eyes when he saw you?"

Marcee nodded. He *had* seemed pleased to see her. But for her, seeing Sam was harder than she'd ever imagined. When she made her vow to be man-free for this next year, she'd never expected to be confronted with the ultimate temptation. But she was strong. This was her time to find herself, and no handsome sheriff was going to derail her resolve.

Marcee stared at her brother. "You can't leave yet."

Tom brushed a strand of limp brown hair back from his face. Everything about him looked tired, from the dark circles under his eyes to the lines of fatigue on his face. According to Tom, he and Celia had been working practically around the clock since Marcee had agreed to come to Ellwood, wanting to be ready to leave the minute she arrived. She'd thought it was just a figure of speech.

"Celia wanted an early start." Tom glanced at the clock on the wall. "It's already past eleven. Cam might sleep until noon."

While Marcee realized the logic, she hadn't seen the boy in years and wasn't sure she'd know him if she passed him on the street. Yet Tom wanted to leave Camden without performing so much as a basic introduction and without saying good-bye.

"Wake him," Marcee suggested.

Tom shook his head. "No way. It's like waking a bear from hibernation."

"If you don't care about the position you're putting me in, at least think of Camden," Marcee said.

"Celia *really* wants to get going—"

The sound of a horn from the driveway cut off his words.

Tom smiled apologetically. "We have a long drive ahead of us."

"Go ahead." Irritation edged Marcee's voice. Suddenly she couldn't wait to be rid of both her brother and Little Miss Horn Blower. "I'll introduce myself and tell him good-bye from you."

A wave of relief washed across Tom's face. "Thanks, Marcee."

He raised his arms as if to hug her but Marcee took a step back, still irritated with him.

Tom let his hands drop to his sides and with a shrug reached down and grabbed a small cooler packed with food. "I owe you."

"Yes, you do," Marcee agreed. "And one of these days I'm going to collect."

Another honk of the horn spurred Tom into action. With his free hand, he opened the door. But instead of going outside immediately, he paused. "Old man Cronkite and his wife still live to the east. They're in their eighties now and pretty frail. There's a new guy in the house where Don and Margie Wolfe used to live. His daughter and Camden have really hit it off. If you need help, he'd probably be your best bet."

The horn sounded again, and with an unexpected brush of his lips against Marcee's cheek, Tom slipped through the door and was gone. A few seconds later Marcee heard the U-Haul pull out of the drive and head down the street.

She glanced around the kitchen. Even though it had been almost fifteen years, the place still looked the same. The worn linoleum. The teapot wallpaper. She exhaled a ragged breath. So much had happened in this room. It was where her stepfather told her to leave and not come back. Where her mother stood silent when she had needed her support. Where—

The door to the kitchen opened without warning and a tall lanky male with a shock of red hair ambled into the room.

Barefoot and wearing gray sweatpants and a faded green T-shirt with the slogan DOESN'T PLAY WELL WITH OTHERS, the boy looked like he'd just rolled out of bed.

"Mornin'," he said, giving her a jerky nod on his way to the cupboard.

Marcee opened her mouth to say hello but shut it when she realized the boy wasn't paying attention. Instead he was digging through the cupboard with single-minded determination. Obviously greeting his long lost half sister didn't interest him half as much as finding what he was looking for in a cabinet filled with an assortment of breakfast cereals.

Marcee sat down at the table and studied him over the rim of her coffee cup as he pulled boxes out then shoved them back into place.

He was tall—at least six feet—with a gangly skinniness that made him look more boy than man. His face was all sharp angles with a smattering of freckles topped off by a mop of disheveled dark red curls.

Marcee narrowed her gaze. The boy reminded her of someone. She thought for a moment. A young Carrot Top? Yes, that was it. If Camden's hair had been any lighter, he would have been the spitting image of the popular comedian.

Of course, there were differences. Carrot Top was always making jokes and laughing. From the determined look on Camden's face, her brother wasn't finding much humor in his current situation. And then there was the matter of his eyebrow. The last time Marcee had seen Carrot Top in Las Vegas, she didn't remember him having any piercings.

"Celia," Camden bellowed unexpectedly without turning around. "Where'd you hide the pop tarts?"

"She's gone," Marcee said matter-of-factly, placing her coffee cup back on the table.

He whirled, his brows pulling together.

Marcee met his gaze, surprised to discover his eyes were as green as hers.

"They left?" The boy pinned Marcee with a look. "Already?"

His voice cracked but Marcee pretended not to notice. She lifted one shoulder in a slight shrug.

"Can't say I'm sorry to hear she's gone." Camden took a few steps, pulled out a chair and plopped into it. "Tom's okay, but Celia . . . "

The boy's exaggerated shudder brought a smile to Marcee's lips. His openness made her feel as if she was talking to an old friend, yet they hadn't even been introduced. "By the way, I'm—"

"I know who you are," Cam said before she could finish. "My new watchdog."

His words held an undercurrent she couldn't quite identify.

"I prefer to think of myself as your new house-mate," Marcee said.

Camden leaned back in his chair and his eyes took on an assessing gleam.

She met his gaze and stared right back.

"Why'd you do it?" he asked finally.

"Do what?"

"Why'd you leave a cool place like Chicago to come here?"

His intonation told her exactly what he thought of his hometown, and the realization that their similarities went beyond skin deep made her smile. "What did Tom tell you?"

"That you were between jobs and needed a place to stay."

A wave of irritation washed over Marcee. Damn Tom for making her sound like some sort of destitute street person.

"I came here because I thought it was time you and I got acquainted," Marcee said.

"So coming here was an altruistic gesture," Cam said.

Startled to hear such a comment from a

seventeen-year-old boy, for a moment Marcee could only stare. Had she even known what the word *altruistic* meant when she was his age?

"Let's just say my being here works out for both of us."

Apparently satisfied, Camden's gaze swept over her, lingering on the sleeveless cotton sweater that clung to her chest. He grinned. "I was going to say that we look alike, but from what I can see, there are some *major* differences."

Marcee found herself smiling back. "Yeah," she said. "Like you're wearing more jewelry than I am."

She raised a finger and tapped her brow.

He laughed. "I had it done a couple days ago. Celia screamed when she saw it."

From his pleased look, his sister-in-law's reaction had been an extra bonus.

Marcee's stomach rumbled, telling her that one scone hadn't been enough. She fleetingly considered her suitcases still needing to be unpacked, but decided food took precedence. "How about we go somewhere and grab lunch? Get better acquainted."

To Marcee's surprise, instead of jumping on the offer, Cameron hesitated.

"My treat," she said, sweetening the deal.

After a long moment he shook his head. "I can't. A friend and I are going to the lake today and I promised her I'd be over by noon."

Marcee's discerning ears immediately picked up on the fact that Camden's friend was a girl. And not just any girl, one he didn't want to disappoint.

He pushed back his chair and rose to his feet. "I'm going to make myself a grilled peanut butter sandwich. Want one?"

Without waiting for an answer, he stepped to the stove and pulled a large pan from the drawer beneath the oven.

"You'll love it," he said, apparently taking her silence for assent. "Tom and I could only make it when Celia wasn't home. The skeleton thought it had too many calories."

Marcee's lips twitched at his reference to his sister-in-law's ultrathin frame. She opened her mouth to say she wasn't a fan of peanut butter anything, but swallowed the words before they passed her lips. Something in Camden's eyes told her this offer was his way of welcoming her, and if she rejected the peanut butter, he might think she was rejecting him. It was something she absolutely didn't want to do.

She already liked this seventeen-year-old male

version of herself. Liked his "to hell with you" fashion sense. Liked the keen intelligence that shone in his eyes. But most of all liked the fact that, in his own way, he was trying to make her feel welcome.

The boy whistled under his breath as he sprayed the skillet with nonstick spray and turned on the stove. After pulling out four slices of bread, he slathered them with margarine followed by a thick spread of creamy peanut butter. Celia was right. She'd have to run *five* miles today to make up for the calories . . .

"Something wrong?" Cam asked, and she realized her under-the-breath groan must have been audible.

Marcee sighed. "I was just thinking about all the unpacking I have to do."

"I'll be gone all afternoon," Cam said, his shoulders suddenly stiff, his back ramrod straight. "I won't be in your way."

Something in the way he said the words made Marcee wonder if that's how he'd felt in the past. First in his mother's way, then in Tom and Celia's . . .

"No worries," Marcee said. "I'm the intruder. This is your home, not mine."

Cam expertly flipped the sandwiches, then

turned, spatula in hand. "This was your home once."

"That was a long time ago," she said, keeping her tone deliberately light.

"Would you ever consider moving back permanently?" he asked unexpectedly.

"Nope."

"That's what I thought," Cam said. "You're way too cool for this town."

Marcee found herself smiling. She liked the kid. Who wouldn't like someone with such discerning taste? "I bet your girlfriend is cool, too."

She wasn't sure what made her try to pump him for information but the words slipped out before she could stop them.

His expression turned inscrutable. "What girlfriend?"

"The one you're taking to the lake."

"She's not my girlfriend, she's a *friend*." With each word, Camden's voice rose.

Stunned by the intensity of his response, Marcee's eyes widened. Obviously this subject was one of *his* hot buttons. "I didn't mean—"

Cam slapped the sandwich on a plate like it was a bug he'd like to squash and placed it in front of her. "I don't want you talking to the neighbors, telling them she's my girlfriend, when she's not."

A swath of color splashed across his cheeks. "She and I are just friends."

They might only be friends, but the vehemence of Camden's denial told Marcee he obviously wished there could be more. Regardless, the boy didn't need to worry about her.

"I may have been gone a long time," Marcee said, "but I remember what it's like. I won't talk about you to other people, and I'd appreciate it if you did the same."

Cam snorted, and she took that as agreement.

She relaxed back in her chair and a pleased smile lifted her lips. It was obvious she and Camden were on the same wavelength. Suddenly, surviving the year didn't seem so daunting a task.

Camden would do his thing. She would do hers. And as long as she kept her distance from Sam McKelvey, they should all be fine.

By the time suppertime rolled around, Marcee had unpacked her suitcases, familiarized herself with the house, and watched two hours of daytime television. It was six o'clock and she didn't expect Camden back for hours.

Restless, she moved to the front window and

peered through the lace curtains. The bright sun of a few hours ago had been replaced by clouds. She went to the door and stuck out her head. A light breeze caressed her cheek, and the heat of the day had started to ease.

Perfect weather for a run.

In less than ten minutes she had pulled on a pair of gym shorts and a tiny tee, stuck iPod buds in her ears and was out the door. Instead of heading down the street, she turned south at the corner. After several blocks she found the bike trail that circled the town. She had no doubt that in less than an hour it would be crowded with bikes and rollerblades and slow-moving seniors. But right now she had it all to herself.

She'd gone about a mile when someone grabbed her from behind. Her heart jumped to her throat and she jerked back, breaking free. Unfortunately the force threw her off balance.

Marcee fought to right herself but the concrete path loomed. Then the same strong arm reached out and grabbed her again. She pushed herself back, prepared to fight for her life. But when she came face-to-face with familiar hazel eyes, the fight went out of her and the breath she'd been holding came out in a whoosh. "Ohmygod, Sam."

"I called out to you," he said, his eyes filled with

concern. "But you kept going. When I touched your arm . . . I think I scared you."

"I was so freaked." With trembling hands, Marcee pulled the buds from her ears and shoved them in her pocket. "Even now, I can't stop shaking."

"I'm sorry." He pulled her to him and held her close.

Marcee rested her head against his chest, finding comfort in the steady beat of his heart. Though she told herself to pull away, she didn't move a muscle.

"Are you sure you're okay?" Sam whispered against her hair. "You're still trembling."

"It's your fault," she murmured against his chest. "You're wearing the same aftershave you had on when we made love."

His body tightened against her and she realized with sudden horror what she'd said. Dear God, she might as well have stripped off her clothes, lain spread-eagle on the path and said, "Take me."

When an ache of longing to do just that washed over her, Marcee knew she had to take a step back . . . now. He didn't want her, and sex was no longer enough. She placed her hands flat against his chest and pushed.

He released her but stood staring at her with glittery eyes.

"I don't know what got into me." She shifted from one leg to the other, still feeling off balance. "I must have been dazed from the fall."

"You didn't fall," Sam reminded her, a bemused smile lifting his lips. "I caught you."

"Very chivalrous."

He chuckled. "I'm that kind of guy."

And that's what made him so dangerous.

"Well, thank you." Marcee brushed back a strand of hair that had come loose from her pony-tail. "I'd better start running. Before it begins to rain . . . and all."

"It's going to be hard." His eyes never left her face. "Pretending I don't know you."

For a second she wasn't sure what he meant. Then it hit her. "I didn't mean you have to act like we didn't know each other. I just meant not to let people know we know each other."

Marcee paused. She'd graduated from North-western with a minor in English, and there was something definitely wrong with that sentence. "I think I just used 'know' three times."

"Actually, four." The dimple in his cheek flashed. "But who's counting?"

"You know what—" Marcee stopped herself and began to laugh.

The deep timbre of his laughter mingled with

hers. And though she wasn't quite sure how it happened, the tension between them dissolved and once again they were back on comfortable ground.

"You," she paused, "*understand* what I'm trying to say."

A grin tugged at the corners of his lips. "I believe you meant 'to know' in the biblical sense. Am I on the right track?"

Marcee nodded, relieved she didn't have to try and explain it again.

"That I can do," Sam said. "I hope you realize the warning wasn't necessary. I've never been one to kiss and tell."

Marcee stared into his eyes and could see the truth of his words in the liquid depths. "I just needed to make sure."

"Don't worry for a minute." Sam reached out, and for a moment she thought he was going to touch her face. Instead he gently tucked the troublesome strand of hair behind her ear. "I'll take my lead from you. If you want to just be friends, that's what it will be."

Friends? No, she didn't want to be his friend, she wanted . . . no *needed* to go back to being strangers. Even friends could be too tempting.

" . . . my neighbor," he said.

She pulled her thoughts back to the present and realized that while she'd been contemplating the perils of friendship he'd been talking. "What did you say about your neighbor?"

"I said I didn't realize you lived next door until I saw you leave the house."

"*You* bought Don and Margie Wolfe's home?"

"Don't sound so horrified," Sam said with a grin. "Most people find the thought of having a sheriff next door rather comforting."

Next door. The only thing worse would be . . . Surely not. But once the thought took hold it wouldn't go away. She simply had to ask. "Is your bedroom on the second floor, southwest corner?"

"As a matter of fact it is." Sam lifted a brow. "Why?"

"No reason." A feeling of dread curled tight in her stomach.

"There *is* a reason or you wouldn't have brought it up."

"Putting those detective skills to good use I see," Marcee said. "Do you get much chance to use those in Ellwood?"

"I'm using them now," he said, his voice filled with amusement. "Answer the question."

Marcee hesitated for a long moment.

"If you must know," she said finally. "My room is on the second floor north. If I look out my window I can see right into yours."

"Unless I have the blinds closed."

She breathed a sigh of relief. "Of course."

"But the blinds won't be closed."

Marcee's mouth went dry. "They won't?"

"No." Sam took a step forward. "I like the idea of you watching me. It'll be almost as if you're in the room with me."

Her knees went weak but she forced a nonchalant smile. "How do you know I'll be looking?"

He met her gaze and she could feel the electricity all the way down to her toes. "You'll be looking."

A crack of thunder rumbled overhead, warning her she'd lingered too long. She glanced up and saw that the gray sky had turned black. "I better head home."

She didn't wait for his reply but turned back in the direction she'd come. But she'd barely taken a step when his hand closed over her arm.

"I never got a good-bye kiss," he said. "When I left the hotel room."

He was right. She hadn't kissed him. Though there had been plenty of kissing throughout the night, when it came time for him to leave, she'd kept her lips to herself. It had been harder than she'd imagined, letting him go, knowing she would never seen him again.

He'd given her his number but never asked for hers. Though she acted cool about it, it had given him the control. That's why when he'd reached for her at the door, she smiled, stepped back and shut the door—not really in his face, but close.

She gave a little shrug as if the matter was of no consequence. "So?"

"If we're going to move on," he said, "I think we need closure."

Just like in the hotel room, a curious humming filled her body even as she pretended not to understand. "What do you mean?"

He took a step closer and lifted her chin with the curve of his fingers. "One last kiss."

Red flags popped up in such rapid succession that Marcee felt dizzy. Warning bells rang like gongs in her head. Perhaps she should have paid them some heed, but he wasn't asking her to sleep with him, he only wanted a good-bye kiss . . . a reasonable request. And as he'd said, a way to put some closure on that night in the hotel.

"Okay, one last kiss." She slipped her arms around his neck. "For closure."

She expected his lips to immediately close

over hers. Instead, with a relieved sigh, he pulled her to him, holding her tight. "Ah, Red. I've missed you."

The words and the emotion in them tugged at her heart, and a frisson of fear shot up her spine. His good-bye, Marcee realized, was starting to feel a whole lot more like hello.

Sam couldn't have said how long he stood on that deserted path with Marcee in his arms. He only knew how right and good it felt.

She was soft and warm and her hair smelled like jasmine. Despite knowing he was playing with fire by embracing a woman in public—it would probably be newsworthy enough to make the front page of the *Ellwood Gazette*—he couldn't bring himself to release her.

Yet, while he wanted nothing more than to taste the sweetness of her lips, the knowledge that this kiss would bring *closure* made him hold back. On the other hand, thinking they could continue what they'd begun back in that ballroom in Chicago was simple foolishness.

He tightened his hold on her and she shifted, her body molding against his, reminding him how perfectly they'd fit together that night in the hotel.

She lifted her face to his, and he saw the same need that coursed hot through his veins reflected in the emerald depths.

A deep rumble rolled overhead, but he ignored the warning and slid his hands down her back. If this was to be the last time they kissed, he intended to make it one she'd never forget. But before his lips had a chance to even brush hers, a plop of rain hit her brow and she jerked back. Then another drop hit. And another. The droplets were soon coming so fast it was hard to tell where one ended and the next began.

A crack of thunder rent the air, and Sam realized they had to find shelter. In seconds the heavens would open up and they'd be drenched. He grabbed Marcee's hand and they began to run. After about fifty yards she released his hand and sprinted ahead. Sam increased his pace, matching her step for step.

"Nice evening for a run," he said, raising his

voice so she could hear him above the crack of thunder.

"Refreshing," Marcee agreed.

"Do you do this often?" he asked, his breath coming in short puffs.

"Run in the rain?"

He grinned. "No, run . . . jog . . . sprint."

Though his lungs were burning, the beautiful redhead at his side didn't appear a bit short of breath. She made it look effortless.

"I try to run every day," she said, picking up the pace as they ran down the street and the rain fell harder. "I have since high school. Back then I was a real jock. I still hold the Ellwood High 3200 meter record."

Sam struggled to keep up. He'd always thought he was in good shape, but it looked like he was going to need to vary his workout to include more treadmill time. "Never pegged you as an athlete."

Marcee glanced at him and gave him a wink without breaking stride. "There's more to me than meets the eye."

That, Sam realized, was a serious understatement.

"This way." She punched his arm, and he turned

his head just in time to see her veer toward a building, to take shelter beneath a large overhang.

He followed, then doubled over, his hands on his thighs as he caught his breath.

"Someone needs to work on endurance," Marcee teased.

Sam couldn't help but laugh. "I think you're right."

He straightened and raked his hand through his wet hair. His shirt and running shorts were plastered to his body and he had the feeling his shoes would squish if he took another step. "What a pair we make," he said with a self-deprecating grin. "Couple of drowned rats."

"Speak for yourself, lawman." Marcee chuckled, flashing a smile. "I prefer to think of myself as being gently kissed by the rain."

Her water-soaked tee clung to her large breasts, while her shorts molded against her firm derriere. Sam lifted his gaze to her luscious lips, consumed by the urge to taste.

He reached for her, but when he stepped forward she moved a step back and gave her head an almost imperceptible shake. "We're being watched."

Sam stilled and let his hand drop to his side. "Where?"

"Across the street. Yellow house, front window."

Trying not to be obvious, Sam slanted a gaze in that direction. She was right. Through the falling rain he could see a tall figure in one of the houses, behind a picture window, too far away to make out details. He narrowed his gaze. "Looks like they have . . . binoculars?"

Marcee laughed. "Wouldn't surprise me one bit."

Sam found the idea that someone could be so nosy irritating as hell. "There goes our kiss."

"Guess closure will have to wait," Marcee said, sounding not at all disturbed by the delay.

For a second he wondered if he'd misread the electricity sizzling between them. Then he caught sight of the nipples straining against fabric, noticed the pulse beating rapidly in the silky curve of her neck, and saw the heat in her gaze. No, he realized with a flash of relief, she wanted him, she just had self-control.

Sam forced his gaze from her and studied the structure that had given them shelter. It was an odd building, smaller than the homes surrounding it. Two large plate-glass windows flanked the front door, and the large overhang that protected them from the rain extended almost all the way to the street. A slightly askew For Sale sign hung in the window.

"What did this place used to be?" he asked. "Do you know?"

"When I lived here it was called the Little Giant," Marcee said, a smile of remembrance lifting her lips. "It was very popular. All the high school kids hung out here."

"What did they sell?"

"The place was a forerunner of the modern convenience store," Marcee said. "They sold candy and drinks and homemade baked goods. In the summer there were tables right here, under the overhang."

Sam glanced around the neighborhood. One thing didn't jive. "This is a residential area."

"And this is a small town." Marcee's lips quirked upward. "Zoning laws aren't as stringent. Or at least they didn't use to be."

She moved to the window behind them and pressed her face against the glass, peering inside. "I wonder where kids go now?"

Sam pressed his lips together, remembering the skimpy bikini his daughter had insisted on wearing. "Your brother took Fern to the lake."

Marcee turned and narrowed her gaze. "Do you have something against my brother?"

Her voice had taken on an edge, warning him to tread lightly. But he'd never lied to Marcee and wasn't about to start now. "It's not Camden," he said. "It's just that I don't want my daughter getting serious about *any* boy."

"Serious?" Marcee laughed. "You've only been in town a month. How serious can they be?"

Sam knew it didn't make sense, but his gut told him Fern's feelings for Camden went far beyond casual friendship. "Fern really likes him. I know she says they're only friends, but—"

"Fern's a pretty girl," Marcee said. "Surely she's dated before?"

"Of course," Sam said. "But no one steadily."

He barely remembered any of their names. What he did recall was the breezy attitude Fern had about all of them.

"When she talks about Cam, there's a different look in her eyes." Sam threw up his hands, realizing he sounded like an overprotective father, but unable to stop himself, he added, "It concerns me."

Marcee tilted her head. "Do you think they're sleeping together?"

"Dear God, no," he blurted, then realized she'd struck at the heart of his fear. He raked his hand through his hair. "At least I don't think so . . . I hope not."

"She *is* seventeen," Marcee said softly. "Lots of girls are having sex at that age."

"She's a child."

"A young woman," Marcee said. "You probably weren't much older than her when you were married."

A knot formed in the pit of his stomach. Surely Fern wouldn't make the same mistake he had. He'd been eighteen when he and Laura married. "I was nineteen when Fern was born."

Marcee's gaze searched his. "Any regrets?"

"A few," he said, feeling disloyal to Laura for even admitting that much. "But I wouldn't change a thing," he hastened to add. "Fern has been such a blessing."

"Yet you don't want her going down the same path . . . "

Sam hesitated. Didn't every parent want more for their child than the life they'd had? "I want to see her get through high school, go on to college and enjoy life. Not have to bear the weight of too many responsibilities before her time."

"Like you did?"

Sam saw the speculative look in Marcee's eyes. But it seemed that to say more about his relationship with Laura wouldn't be fair to his wife's memory. Whatever her faults, Laura had been a good wife and mother. So instead of answering, he shifted his gaze to the street. "Looks like the rain is finally letting up."

"Saved by the weather," Marcee said, but the understanding in her eyes told him she was through prying . . . at least for now.

"I suppose we should take advantage of the lull and make a break for it," she said.

But Sam didn't want to leave. This was their little world; under the overhang with the rain gently falling all around them. Where nothing existed, nothing mattered, except for Marcee.

His gaze locked with hers.

"The person with the binoculars hasn't moved." Marcee spoke softly though there was no one nearby. "Now that the rain has stopped, he, or she, has an even better view."

Sam wanted to say that he didn't care, let them look. He wanted to pull her into his arms and kiss her until her blood ran hot and she begged him to make love to her. But he knew that would be foolhardy and have disastrous consequences. "Appears closure will have to wait."

Marcee just smiled. "People say patience is a virtue."

"I've heard that," Sam muttered. "Not sure I believe it."

"I'm not sure I buy it, either." She grinned. "Race you home?"

They started running again, and this time he kept up, matching her stride for stride. He inhaled the fresh evening air and found himself enjoying simply being with her. Maybe being patient *was* a good thing. Because it meant, at least for now, that the bond between him and the beautiful red-head would remain unbroken.

The radio was blaring a classical piece when Marcee walked through the kitchen door. Cam sat at the table with a Coke and a bowl of chips, intently studying a piece of sheet music.

She stopped just inside the door, reached over and shut off the radio. Then she untied her shoes and kicked them off before peeling away her wet socks. "How long have you been home?"

Cam glanced up. "About an hour. We left the lake as soon as the lightning started."

"Where's Fern?"

She saw Camden's shoulders tense. He turned in his seat. "How did you know I was with Fern?"

"I ran into her dad on the bike path," Marcee said. "Actually, I knew Sam and Fern when I lived in Chicago. When he said he lived next door, I made the connection."

Cam didn't say a word but she could feel his irritation all the way across the room.

Now barefoot, Marcee padded across the weathered linoleum and plopped down in the chair opposite him at the table. "If you have something you want to say to me, say it."

He lifted his gaze. "You talked to *him* about Fern. And me."

"We talked about my move to Ellwood." Marcee spoke slowly and deliberately so there would be no misunderstanding. "That's when I discovered they were our neighbors and figured out that Fern is the girl you've been seeing."

"Not seeing," Cam clarified. "Friends."

"Her father thinks that it's more than that."

"How scary for him." Cam pretended to shudder, then met Marcee's gaze. "He doesn't like me. Never has."

While Cam did a great job of concealing his emotions, Marcee could hear the hurt underlying the words. "Once Sam has a chance to know you better that will change."

He shrugged. "I'm not losing sleep over it."

"Another thing we have in common," she said, keeping her tone light. "The parents of the guys I dated in high school never liked me, either."

She'd expected Cam to protest that he wasn't

dating Fern, but instead he tilted his head. "Why do you think that was?"

Rather than tossing off some quick one-liner, Marcee took a moment to consider the question. "I think they were terrified I'd lead their sons astray."

It was amusing now, but at the time their attitude had done a number on her self-esteem. Marcee pushed to her feet and took a couple steps to the ancient refrigerator. She pulled a can of soda from the cool depths before returning to the table. "In a way, it was funny, because I thought I was a good kid. On the honor roll. Didn't smoke. Or do drugs."

"They must have had some reason for disliking you." Cam shoved the sheet music aside, giving her his full attention.

"Shirleen was a factor," Marcee admitted. "She wasn't exactly a pillar of the community, not with her revolving door of men."

"That hasn't changed." Cam's lips quirked upward. "You should have heard the buzz when she brought Mad Dog back with her from Sturgis."

"I can only imagine." Marcee munched on a chip. "She's a magnet for losers."

For a moment Marcee hesitated, remembering

her vow not to bad-mouth or gossip. But these were facts, not gossip.

"My dad was one," Cam said.

"Mine, too," Marcee admitted.

"Any idea where yours is?"

"Nope," she said. "He disappeared right after Shirleen filed for divorce. Haven't seen him since I was seven. The funny thing was, I actually missed him when I was a kid."

"I used to dream about my dad coming back . . . now I look back and think, geez, was I crazy?" He gave a bark of a laugh.

"It's a fantasy kind of thing," Marcee said with a shrug. "We all want a normal family. But for you and I, well, it just wasn't in the cards."

Cam seemed to mull the idea over. He finally nodded and picked up a chip. "Was Mom the only reason those parents didn't like you?"

"Her and these." Marcee pointed a finger at her chest.

Sam paused mid-crunch then choked down a swallow. "They didn't like you 'cause you had big boobs?"

"Crazy but true," Marcee said. "Like I said before, they were afraid I'd lead their sons into temptation."

Cam's eyes darkened. "Stupid."

"I didn't care—" Marcee stopped. She'd lied to herself and to others for so many years that by now skirting troublesome truths had become second nature. But part of becoming a better person was being an honest one. "It hurt. But I have to admit I rather enjoyed playing the vamp card when it suited my purposes."

"Vamp card?" Cam's brows pulled together. "You lost me."

"You know, talking sexy, showing a little skin, flirting outrageously."

"You gave them what they expected."

"Exactly."

"Not the smartest move."

"Never said it was."

Cam was silent for a long moment. "I guess I can understand. I got this," he pointed to the metal piercing his brow, "because Celia was always calling me 'alternative.' What the heck does that even mean?"

"I'm starting to realize that you and I are a lot alike." It wasn't necessarily a positive, but still, the realization warmed Marcee's heart. She and Tom had always had an amicable relationship but they'd never really connected. "I'm telling you right now that we're both going to be successful.

In spite of our crummy parents and screwed-up childhoods, we are going to come out on top. And we are going to be happy."

At the empowerment seminar, there'd been a lot of talk regarding the power of positive affirmation. Marcee had been tempted to dismiss what was said as just a bunch of psychological mumbo-jumbo. But now, saying the words out loud, seeing the answering flare in Cam's eyes and feeling her own resolve strengthen, she realized there *was* power in words.

"I want to go to Juilliard," Cam said. "I've always wanted to go there. Before he left, Tom helped me fill out the application and we went over the financial aid stuff. But it's really hard to get in."

"It will happen," Marcee said, gripping his arm and staring into the green eyes that were so like her own. "Because you, Camden Smith, are going to make it happen."

"I'll try—" Cam said, then stopped at the look in Marcee's eye, "No, I will make it happen."

She nodded. "The only thing you'll have to watch out for is romantic complications. I know you're not dating anyone right now but it's something to keep in mind for the future. An unwanted pregnancy could seriously impact your plans."

Dear God, what craziness had come over her? Did she want to have a birds and bees talk with a teenager?

To her surprise, Cam didn't appear embarrassed or offended. "I'm not stupid. If I was dating someone and we were having sex, I'd make sure we used protection." His voice softened. "Because that's what a man does . . . he takes care of and protects those he loves."

Staring into her half brother's intense green eyes, Marcee realized that at seventeen he was more grown-up than most men twice his age.

Sam McKelvey had no reason to worry. Not as long as Camden Smith was in his daughter's life.

The rest of the evening passed quickly. Marcee and Cam made a pizza then watched a movie. By eleven o'clock he was at the computer and she headed upstairs.

After stopping to take a quick shower, Marcee headed to her room. Though she'd told herself she wouldn't look, the moment she crossed the threshold her eyes strayed to the window facing the McKelvey house. Even from across the room she could see that the lights were on and the shades open.

Cinching the belt to her robe, she moved with sure, firm steps to the window. One quick pull and her shade would be down. Temptation would be out of sight.

Her fingers curved around the pull but she couldn't seem to give it a tug. Maybe just one quick peek . . .

She saw Sam immediately. He was sitting in a chair to the left of the window reading the newspaper.

After a long moment, she slipped her hand into her pocket and pulled out her phone. Tearing her eyes away from Sam, she glanced down and scrolled to his number, the one he'd given her all those months ago. Before she could change her mind, she hit speed dial.

The windows were open and she could hear the ring of his phone echo in the clear night air. He looked up and caught her staring at the same time he flipped his phone open.

"You kept my number," he said, a smile creasing his lips. "I'm flattered."

"As far as I'm concerned, every single woman should have at least one police officer on speed dial," Marcee said.

He put the paper aside, stood and moved to the window. Even in black gym shorts and a gray T-shirt, he cut a commanding figure. "Is this a 911 call?" he asked. "Just say the word and in thirty seconds I'm there. I won't even need to use the front door. I'm great at climbing a trellis."

Marcee laughed. "Now that, I'd like to see."

"I know what I'd like to see," Sam said, and she swore she saw his eyes glitter. "Are you naked beneath that robe?"

Goose bumps covered her body. "Maybe."

"I remember how you looked that night," he said. "I bet you'd look even more beautiful now in the moonlight."

"Very smooth, Sheriff." Though desire hot and insistent rose up inside her, Marcee kept her tone light.

"It would be just between you and me. You can't see into either of our windows from the street," Sam added. "I checked on the way home."

"And you're very thorough," Marcee added.

Even across the span between the two houses, Marcee could feel his heat, feel the pull. What would it hurt? Her fingers moved to the belt of her robe, tugging at the knot.

She lowered her gaze and saw the bracelet. Her hand stilled. No. She would stay strong. She wouldn't give in to her desires. Not until she figured out how he fit into her life.

It took all her strength, but she lifted her hand to the shade. "We have to stop this craziness."

"No, we don't."

"We're friends, Sam, just friends."

"So?"

"Friends don't let friends see them naked."

Before she could change her mind, Marcee pulled down the shade and hung up the phone.

Marcee took a step back, placed her hands on her hips and surveyed the brightly colored lights she'd strung around the deck. Though it wouldn't be dark for several hours, she'd turned them on. She nodded in satisfaction. The lights definitely added a festive air.

Having a party had been Iris's suggestion; going with a Mexican theme had been her own idea. Adding to the atmosphere were brightly colored dishes and salsa music playing on the boom box.

The guest list had been kept deliberately small. According to Iris, this was a way for her to dip her toe back into Ellwood society. Two former friends from high school and their husbands were coming, along with Marcee, Iris, and two men.

Marcee pressed her lips together. Just that afternoon Iris had just sprung the fact that she was bringing two guys with her. When she'd told her that she hadn't planned on having a date, Iris laughed and said it wasn't like that at all. Apparently, one of the men was the new city prosecutor and the other was his cousin, visiting from Maine. They'd been in the bakery lamenting the lack of things to do in Ellwood, and on the spur of the moment Iris invited them.

"Looks like someone is having a party."

Marcee recognized Sam's deep voice immediately, and when she turned toward the deck steps, a welcoming smile was on her lips.

"Hey, stranger." She leaned back against the table, thankful she looked her best. Her makeup had just been freshened and she'd changed from the shorts and T-shirt into a flowing green skirt and white peasant blouse. "Haven't seen you since our run in the rain."

"I know," Sam said with a rueful smile. "This week has been crazy busy."

It had been four days since she'd laid eyes on him, which was unbelievable considering he lived next door. She'd wondered if he was avoiding her, and then Fern had mentioned, when she came over earlier, that she and her dad had spent every evening that week painting her bedroom.

They'd even done all the prep work. Marcee was tempted to ask why they hadn't just hired someone, then saw the look in the girl's eyes and listened to her happy chatter about the experience. If Sam's goal was to build a relationship with his daughter, he was well on his way.

"*Are* you having a party?"

The question broke through her reverie, and Marcee pulled her thoughts back to the present, realizing with a start that Sam now stood beside her. Though he was dressed simply in khaki cargo shorts and a brick-colored T-shirt, her heartbeat picked up. She'd known many handsome men in her lifetime, but none that set her heart beating like this one.

"Iris and I invited some women from high school and their husbands over for an evening of Mexican and margarita madness," she said with a laugh, feeling oddly flustered. "A couple guys Iris knows are apparently stopping by, too."

Surprise widened Sam's hazel eyes for a second and his smile faltered. "I didn't know you were dating."

"I'm not," Marcee said. "Like I said, it's just some guys Iris invited. One of them is the new city prosecutor, Jeff Spence. Do you know him?"

"We've met." Sam's expression gave nothing away, and Marcee's unease grew.

"Okay guy?"

"He's a straight shooter," Sam said almost grudgingly.

The doorbell rang and Marcee jumped. "Looks like they're here."

Though she'd been looking forward to the party, she suddenly wished it could have held off for just a while longer.

"I'd better go," Sam said, but he made no move to leave.

"Why don't you stay?" Marcee asked, keeping her tone casual, resisting an urge to beg. If Sam was here, she knew she'd have a good time. "I'll give you a Corona."

He shook his head. "I'm not going to intrude."

"You wouldn't be." Giving into an overpowering impulse, Marcee touched his arm. "I've missed talking to you."

His gaze searched her face. "Same here."

The air, which had been light and breezy only moments before, turned thick with longing. Sam must have felt it, too, because his eyes darkened.

Marcee held her breath.

The doorbell rang again and the connection shattered.

"You have guests," he said with a smile that didn't quite reach his eyes. "We'll connect another time."

With a sigh, she turned back to the house. She was almost to the sliding glass door when Sam called her name. Whirling, she met his gaze.

"One more thing," he said.

"What's that?"

"Just remember. The light is always on."

"What do you think he meant by that?" Marcee slanted a sideways glance at Iris and grabbed the last chip from a large orange bowl.

After the guests left, Iris stayed behind to help her clean up. They were almost finished when they decided to take a break.

"Leave the light on?" Iris's expression grew thoughtful. "It reminds me of an old commercial for a motel chain. The slogan meant they'd always be there waiting for you."

"I don't think—"

"That's it," Iris said with a triumphant smile, slapping a flat palm against the table. "He's saying he wants you."

Though a little surge of pleasure shot though her at Iris's words, she kept her expression carefully neutral. "I'm sure it's not in *that* way," she said. "He's probably being a good neighbor, letting me know I can count on him."

Marcee wasn't sure why it was so hard for

her to discuss her feelings for Sam with Iris. She didn't doubt Iris's loyalty or her discretion. Still, whatever there was between her and Sam—and she wasn't sure herself what it was—somehow seemed too personal to share.

"I don't understand you."

She looked up to find her friend staring. "What's to understand?"

"For starters, this thing with Sam." Iris leaned back in her chair, her gaze sharp and assessing. "And Jeff. What was that about? It was obvious the guy was crazy about you, yet you didn't give him *any* encouragement."

"He was nice." Easy on the eyes and intelligence would normally be a potent combination. Yes, the city prosecutor definitely had a lot going for him. But when Jeff had teasingly taken her hand at one point during the evening, she hadn't felt a single spark.

"Nice?" Iris screwed her face up. "The man is sizzlin'."

"If you like him so much, why don't you go for him?"

"I've told you, I like my men well done, not rare."

Marcee bit into a chip. "Why is that?"

"Personal preference," Iris said with a dismissive wave. "Besides, we were talking about you, not me."

Marcee laughed. "No," she said pointedly. "We'd moved on to you."

"Well, I'd love to spend a couple hours talking about my ideal man, but unfortunately I don't have time." Iris stood and stretched. "Three A.M. will be here before I know it."

Marcee stood, picked up the rest of the dishes, and followed her friend into the kitchen. "Thanks, Iris."

A puzzled look crossed her friend's face. "For what?"

"For making me have this party," she said. "For reminding me it's not always *where* we are but *who* we're with that makes life enjoyable. I really like hanging out with you."

"Ditto."

The sound of a door slamming shut and heavy footsteps on the stairs punctuated Iris's words. She slanted Marcee a questioning look.

"Camden." Marcee glanced at her watch. Right on time. Her brother had taken Fern to a movie and dinner. Though Cam had complained about Fern's early curfew, he'd gotten her home on time.

"How do you like being a mom?" Iris asked as they walked to the front door.

"I like it," Marcee said, hearing the surprise in her own voice. "Camden is a good kid. He makes it easy."

"He's lucky to have you." Iris's gaze grew pensive. "It's not easy having a mother like Shirleen."

"Tell me about it," Marcee said, her lips twisting in a wry smile. "But the way I look at it, Cam and me, well, we're lucky to have each other."

"You are indeed." Iris reached over and gave her a quick hug. "And remember, if you need anything, you've got a neighbor with his light on."

Marcee just smiled. That wasn't something she was likely to forget.

Sam had been watching the news when he heard the front door open. He expected Fern to call out a greeting then head upstairs. Instead she danced into the room, plopped herself down on the sofa and started to chatter. He heard all about the movie she and Cam had seen. Apparently, the romantic comedy made her cry but Cam had been cool about the tears. She then launched into a review of the Italian restaurant that had just opened in neighboring Berryville.

Sam tried to pay attention, because he knew that moments like these were precious. But his thoughts were still next door. Less than a half hour ago he'd heard the car doors slam and knew Marcee's party was breaking up. Though it was ridiculous, he'd found himself hoping Marcee would call and tell him how it went.

If the laughter that had carried on the night breeze was any indication, her first party in Ellwood had been a rousing success.

He couldn't help wondering what she thought of Jeff Spence, if she liked him. He had no doubt that Jeff had liked her. What wasn't to like? Marcee wasn't only beautiful and smart, but fun to be with as well. Not to mention sexy as hell.

Had Jeff kissed her good-night?

Sam shoved the troubling thought aside, reminding himself for the umpteenth time that Marcee's private life was none of his business.

"Good night, Daddy." Fern brushed a kiss across his cheek. "Love you."

"Love you, too, honey." Sam realized with a flash of guilt that while thinking about Marcee he'd missed the restaurant review. "Fern."

She was already halfway to the stairs, but turned and came back. "Yes, Daddy?"

He stared at her precious features and his heart overflowed with love. He still worried about her dating, but at least the lines of communication were now open. "I had fun painting the room with you this week."

She flashed him a brilliant smile. "Me, too."

Sam heard her humming to herself as she started up the stairs, and his own lips lifted in a smile. Though he hadn't thought about it in years, he remembered how, when Fern was a little girl, she always sang or hummed when she was happy.

Other than that, he didn't remember much about her childhood. Determined to make detective at an early age, he'd pulled double shifts and taken extra assignments. He'd told himself he was doing it for his family . . . but it had been his family—his wife and daughter—who were short-changed. Only recently had he begun to realize all that he'd missed.

He shoved the depressing thoughts aside as he climbed the stairs, his mind returning to Marcee. When he went to her house earlier, he'd hoped to spend some time with her. Talk. Laugh. Relax. He still felt the need for that connection.

Sam flipped on the light in his room and crossed the oak floor to stand at the window. Marcee's room was lit but the shades were drawn.

A friend had once told him that if you're truly

connected to a person, you could communicate without saying a word. He closed his eyes and concentrated. *Open the shade.*

To his surprise, in only seconds the shade was raised and Marcee stood in the window. Their eyes locked and, even across the distance, Sam felt the jolt.

She'd never looked more beautiful. In the moonlight, with her hair hanging loose to her shoulders, she reminded him of an angel.

Without taking his eyes off her, he pulled the phone from his pocket and dialed her number.

Marcee disappeared for a second then returned with her pink bejeweled phone in hand.

"You left the light on," she said softly.

"I said I would."

"I'm surprised you called," she said. "How did you know Jeff wouldn't be here?"

Though the bluntness of her question took him by surprise, Sam answered honestly. "Because I know you."

He expected her to drop the subject, but for some reason she seemed determined to push the topic. "I let you stay the first night I met you."

"What you and I have is different," he said, daring her to disagree.

"Yes," she admitted in a soft low voice, "it is."

At her words, the tension that had gripped his body left in a whoosh. "How was the party?"

"Fun," she said. "Food was fabulous. Conversation good. But all evening it felt as if something was missing."

Was she intimating that she had missed him? Or was he reading too much into her words, hearing what he wanted her to say?

"Jeff was nice," she continued. "But there was just no spark."

God help him, he couldn't keep the grin from his face. "I take it you're not planning on seeing him again?"

"I didn't say that," Marcee said matter-of-factly, dashing his hopes. "Camden is pretty self-sufficient. Until I decide what I want to do with my life, I have lots of free time."

"Eastside Nursery is hiring," Sam said, recalling a recent conversation with the owner. "I'm not sure if it's for the greenhouse or office. They're a good company, one of the largest in the region."

He clamped his mouth shut before he could do something stupid like offer to pick her up an application. He knew why he'd mentioned the job. If she was busy, she'd have less time to date other men. Of course, to try to hold her to him would be wrong and certainly not fair. Still, the thought of losing her . . . friendship . . . sent a disturbing sense of panic racing though him.

"Hmm." Marcee put a finger to her lips. "I might check it out."

"I'm going to be busy the next few evenings," Sam said. "But I'd like to call you . . . if that's okay?"

"I'd like that," she said. "I'll let you know what I decide to do about the job."

Sam breathed a sigh of relief. It appeared, for now anyway, that everything was back to status quo. He only hoped it stayed that way.

"Medium okay with you?" Deputy Sheriff Ronald Densmore studied the burger on the grill he was tending with an assessing eye before shifting his gaze to Sam.

"Works for me." Sam held out a plate already crowded with potato salad, baked beans, and an oversized sesame bun.

Ron slapped the burger on the bun. "Glad to see you and the kid could make it tonight."

Sam glanced around the backyard. He'd been invited to the monthly cookout shortly after he moved to town. But he was still getting settled then and had declined.

Sponsored by the local Sertoma Club, the cookouts began in May and went through September. This month Ron was hosting the event at his place.

Sam's gaze scanned the crowd. Ron had eight acres on the edge of town, so there was plenty of room for everyone to mingle. Men were pitching horseshoes and drinking beer down by the pole barn, while most of the women stood talking on the patio up by the house. Kids of all ages filled the yard.

There were so many people present that it seemed as if the entire town had decided to show up. Sam had cast a quick glance around the yard when he first arrived, checking out the attendees. The disappointment that washed over him when he failed to spot a single redhead had told him he hadn't been looking for just *anyone*, but a particular *someone*. And he was still hoping to see her.

"Looks like almost everyone in town is here," he said conversationally, waving to his neighbor Joe Martinez down by the horseshoe pit. "Including my neighbors."

Ron's gaze moved away from the grill, following Sam's gesture. "Speaking of neighbors," he said, looking at Sam. "I hear Marcee Robbens moved in next to you."

"That's right," Sam said. "She came back to take

care of her brother while he finishes his senior year."

"I went to school with her." Ron gave a low whistle. "Man, she was some looker. Big tits. Great ass. And don't think she didn't know it."

Sam clenched his jaw tight. While he didn't want to hear Ron talk about Marcee's breasts or her backside, he did want to know if she was going to show up.

They talked on the phone every night and had spoken in person over the backyard fence a couple times. She'd applied for a job at Eastside, but they wouldn't be making their hiring decisions for a couple weeks. To his surprise, she was hoping to work both in the nursery and in the office.

"I don't see her here." Sam said, deciding to play dumb. "Think she'll show?"

"Hope not." Ron popped open a can of beer.

"Why?" He didn't have to feign surprise.

"You've seen her," Ron said.

"Yeah, so . . . " Sam said slowly, wondering what his deputy was getting at, yet not sure he wanted to know.

"Women don't want her around." Ron belched loudly. "Scared she'll get on their husbands."

Sam tightened his grip on his plate. "Why would they think that?"

"'Cuz that's how she is . . . or how she was." Ron ignored the burgers and bratwurst sizzling on the grill, appearing to warm to the topic. "She was wild. Parents kicked her out of the house before she even graduated."

Sam couldn't imagine any parent doing that to a child. His heart twisted at the thought of what it would be like for Fern if she suddenly found herself alone. "How could they do that? She was a child."

"Old enough to screw around," Ron retorted, turning the brats.

Sam pulled his brows together. "What are you talking about?"

"She was babysitting. When her folks came back early, they found her gettin' hot and heavy with her current squeeze while her baby brother was upstairs crying." Ron tilted his head and thought for a moment. "I think the kid might have been hurt. Maybe even bleeding."

Sam tried to hide his shock. That didn't sound like Marcee.

"Anyway, her stepdad blew a gasket," Ron said. "Kicked her slutty ass out of his house faster than you could say 'Put on your clothes, little missy.'"

Sam took a bite of hamburger and forced it past

the sudden dryness in his throat. "What did she do then?"

Ron shrugged. "Stayed with some friends until she graduated. Then she hightailed it out of town, never to be seen again . . . until now."

If what Ron was saying were true, it was pretty damning. Still, Sam felt the need to defend Marcee. "She came back to watch her brother."

Ron laughed. "Don't that beat all? Almost kills the kid and now she's his keeper."

"Fern says they get along well." The minute the words left his mouth, Sam wished he could pull them back. The last thing he wanted to do was add to the gossip, even if it was something positive.

Ron lowered his beer can and his gaze turned sharp and assessing. "Your girl still hangin' out with that good-for-nothin' kid?"

Sam forced himself to take another bite of hamburger and took his time chewing before answering. "He lives next door, Ron. It'd be hard for her *not* to see him."

"I heard they were dating." Ron's eyes gleamed with unabashed interest. "Paula Dees's son Ted said he saw them at the lake together last weekend."

Irritation shot through Sam. Last he knew, hang-

ing out at the lake with a neighbor was no crime
. . . and hardly newsworthy. *Unless,* he reminded
himself, *you lived in Ellwood.*

"I don't think I know Paula," he said, deliberately steering the conversation away from Fern.

"She's high up there in local government."
Ron finished off the last of his beer and flipped
a couple of burgers. "Paula is the administrative
assistant to John Boosalis."

Boosalis was mayor of Ellwood and the man
who'd hired Sam. But Sam had never met Paula.
When he went to the interview, the desk in the
outer alcove had been empty.

"There she is now." Ron waved the spatula in
the air like a banner. "Paula. Over here."

Sam shifted his gaze to find a mid-thirties blonde
winding her way through the crowd. Dressed in
a striped skirt and a blue cotton top with a mod-
est neckline, the woman was pretty, with an all-
American-girl look.

Her smile was friendly without being suggestive, though she did jab Ron playfully in the ribs.

"Next time you want to talk to me, wave me
over or come and get me," she said in a polite but
firm voice. "Don't yell like you're calling one of
your hound dogs."

To Sam's surprise, a splash of color cut a swath across his deputy's cheeks. "C'mon, Paula, don't go gettin' on your high horse. I just wanted you to meet Sam."

Paula paused for a moment as if waiting for Ron to continue. But the deputy must have decided the introductions were complete because he turned his attention back to the grill.

She stepped forward and extended her hand. "I'm Paula Dees, Ron's next door neighbor."

"Sam McKelvey."

Her fingers were soft and cool, but when they touched his, Sam didn't feel the slightest bit of sizzle. It was crazy. Marcee got within ten feet of him and sparks flew. Paula . . . nothing.

"It's nice to meet you," he continued. "I'm surprised I didn't see you when I interviewed."

"I was visiting college campuses with my son Ted," Paula said.

They talked for several minutes, and Sam learned that Paula was a widow with two teenage boys.

"Ted will be a senior," she said. "Jack is just starting high school this year."

"How do they like living in Ellwood?" Sam asked.

Paula had mentioned that she and her late husband had only moved there four years ago, shortly before his death.

"They love it." Pride filled Paula's eyes. "Ted is a starter on both the football and basketball teams, as well as being involved in student government. Jack is still trying to find his niche. Right now he'd rather play video games than do much of anything else."

"My daughter, Fern, will be starting Ellwood High this fall," Sam said. "She's very outgoing so I'm sure it will be fine, but she hasn't had a chance to meet many young people yet—"

"She's going to be a senior, right?"

Sam nodded, not surprised she was aware of that fact. This was Ellwood, after all.

"That's tough, moving so late. If you like, I can have Ted introduce her around," Paula offered. "He's got very nice friends, both boys and girls. If you're like me, even in a small school you know it's important they run with the right crowd—"

"It's nice of you to offer," Sam said, "but I don't want Fern to feel like I'm doing all this arranging behind her back."

"I understand completely." Paula placed her hand on his arm. Still no sizzle. "My boys wouldn't want me doing that to them, either. How about you two come over to dinner sometime next week, say on Thursday? Ted and Fern can meet. What happens after that is up to them."

For a second Sam hesitated, feeling as if he would be disloyal to Marcee if he accepted. Which was crazy, considering this dinner would be just about the kids. "That should work."

"Six o'clock?" Paula asked.

"It's a plan." Sam glanced down at his watch. "Now if you'll excuse me, I need to run."

"Why so early?" Ron asked, confirming what Sam had suspected. The deputy's attention may have appeared to be focused on the burgers and brats, but Ron had heard every word of his conversation with Paula.

"You haven't even finished your supper," Paula added, casting a pointed look at Sam's nearly full plate. "The barbecue is just getting started."

Sam shot a glance toward the rough log where Fern sat talking animatedly with another girl about her age. How could he pull her away now? After all, this evening was as much for her as him.

"C'mon, there are some people I want you to meet." Paula looped her arm companionably through his. "You need to be more social."

Her blue eyes sparkled with good humor, and Sam hesitated only a second before allowing himself to be pulled along. Paula was right. This was a good opportunity for him to meet the citizens of Ellwood in a relaxed setting.

The problem was, he had Marcee on the brain. Not seeing her was driving him crazy. He'd even thought about asking her if she wanted to ride along with him to the party. But he didn't want to share what they had with the citizens of Ellwood . . . not yet anyway.

"I wonder who that is?" Paula said, her tone curious.

Sam pulled his thoughts together and followed Paula's gaze. His heart picked up at the sight of the beautiful redhead standing in the driveway.

Though she was dressed simply in a pair of bright yellow shorts and a white cotton shirt, there was something about Marcee that made her stand out in any crowd. Her hair hung loose to her shoulders, glistening like burnished copper. He remembered the silky feel of those strands between his fingers, and his body stirred. But it was more than her looks that intrigued him.

There was something about the confident set of her shoulders, the proud tilt of her head, and the keen intelligence in her eyes. When coupled with a killer body, it was a potent combination. He could tell the instant she saw him. Her lips lifted, and he couldn't help but smile back, knowing the party could now begin.

"*I don't know why we had to come.*" Cam came to a complete stop at the back of Ron's house and stood looking out over the sea of people, lines of strain around his eyes.

"It'll be fun," Marcee said, though she wasn't sure if it was to reassure him or herself. She waved at the host, noting Ron's stunned expression and the anger that quickly darkened his brow.

Marcee sighed. She'd hoped Ron had matured over the years, but it was obvious that Mr. I'm So Petty I Never Forget a Slight still held those survey results against her. Anywhere else, such a trivial matter would have been long forgotten. Not in Ellwood.

"I gotta tell you," Cam said, his tone surprisingly unsure. "I feel like I'm crashing this party."

"It's just because we don't know very many people," Marcee said. "Or at least, I don't."

When Iris had invited them to the monthly barbecue, Marcee had almost said no. Spend a Saturday night at a small town cookout? No thank you. But before she could graciously refuse, she'd reached for her soda and the lime green bracelet around her wrists had caught her eye.

The way she'd been living her life certainly hadn't made her happy. What did she have to lose by trying something different?

"It's all the food you can eat," she said now, forcing as much enthusiasm into her voice as she could muster. "It'll be fun. Iris assured me there are always lots of teenagers present."

"Yeah," Cam scoffed. "This looks like a happening kind of place."

Marcee cast a sideways glance and saw Camden's lips twitch. Just as she thought—the kid was playing her.

"Trust me." She shot him a wink. "It'll be fun."

He tilted his head and lifted a brow. "Do you think if you say it three times and click your heels, it'll come true?"

Marcee had to laugh. Okay, so maybe she had

repeated herself—a couple times—but she was just trying to maintain a positive outlook. "Yes, I think that's exactly what will happen." She gave him a little shove. "Be off with you, brat. Have fun."

Shifting her gaze back to the partygoers, she scanned the crowd. Some were staring or whispering but most were busy socializing. A few even smiled and lifted a hand in greeting. Startled, Marcee smiled back before returning her gaze to the grassy expanse.

To a casual onlooker her gaze might seem to have skipped indiscriminately across the yard, but she didn't miss a thing. She noticed the men at the horseshoe pit, the children playing badminton . . . and Sam McKelvey at the other side of the yard with a blonde on his arm.

A knot formed in the pit of Marcee's stomach and her smile faltered. She'd assumed Sam was off-duty tonight when she saw Dick patrolling the neighborhood. And she'd figured since his other deputy was the host, it was a good bet that Sam would be at the party tonight. She just hadn't anticipated he'd be here with a *date*.

Marcee tried hard not to glance in the direction of Sam and the blonde. She couldn't believe she'd wasted all afternoon wondering if he was going to ask her to go with him to the barbecue.

Though she told herself now that it didn't matter, her heart twisted.

"I'm going to walk around, check out who's here," Cam said in a suspiciously offhand voice. By the time Marcee glanced in his direction, he was already headed across the yard to where Fern sat on a large hollowed-out log, talking to a brown-haired girl.

Play it cool. Marcee sent the silent warning after him before casting another quick glance in the sheriff's direction. Her mistake was in letting her gaze linger. His gaze captured hers, and even across the vast yard she felt the connection.

Everything faded . . . the kids yelling at the badminton net, the laughter from the women on the patio, the clang of a horseshoe against a metal stake. All she knew was him and that penetrating gaze that seemed to see straight into her soul.

Marcee shivered, feeling more naked than she'd ever felt with her clothes off. It was an unsettling sensation. One she didn't particularly like. Especially when she realized with sudden horror that Sam was coming toward her. And he was bringing the woman with him.

Play it cool, she repeated to herself, lifting her chin and widening her smile to include the woman. She was proud of the fact that no one watching her now would guess that there had ever been anything intimate between her and Sam. Or realize that she was disturbed to discover he was here with a woman.

Sam stopped a few feet in front of her. His smile was easy and his manner relaxed. "What a pleasant surprise."

Marcee wasn't sure what she'd expected him to do—or even say—yet his voice was warm and the welcome in his eyes appeared genuine. He was dressed casually. The western cut of his blue button-up shirt emphasized his broad shoulders, and his faded jeans hugged his lean hips and muscular legs.

She swallowed a sigh. No doubt about it, the man looked yummy enough to eat. But she needed to remember that she wasn't feasting at that buffet. She glanced at her bracelet, took a deep breath, and offered a friendly smile to both Sam and the woman at his side.

Dressed more formally than the occasion dictated, the woman reminded Marcee of a Stepford wife. Not a strand of blond hair was out of place, her coral lipstick was perfectly applied, and her linen skirt didn't have a single crease.

Marcee waited for Sam to perform the introductions. When all he did was continue to stare at her, she shifted her gaze to the blonde and held out her hand.

"I'm Marcee Robbens," she said. "I don't think we've met."

"I don't believe we have," the woman said, her hand closing briefly over Marcee's, her smile open and friendly. "Paula Dees."

"Paula is Ron's neighbor," Sam said quickly, as if realizing his etiquette faux pas. "Marcee is *my* neighbor," he added. "Just moved in last week."

Paula shot Sam a teasing smile. "Well, I hope you properly welcomed her to the neighborhood."

"I did my best." Sam's hazel-eyed gaze locked with Marcee, and though his lips didn't so much as curve in the merest hint of a smile, her legs turned to rubber.

Just his nearness and the scent of his spicy aftershave brought the memories of the one night they'd shared front and center.

"What do you think of our little corner of the world?" Paula leaned forward with something that looked like true interest in her baby blues.

"You know, I've lived here before, and coming back has been interesting," Marcee said diplomatically, then gestured toward a picnic table a few steps away. "Do you mind if we sit? These heeled sandals are killing my feet."

Sam's gaze immediately dropped to her feet. Thankfully, her toenails were freshly polished. She watched his gaze linger on her shapely ankles, peruse her toned calves and thighs before coming to a halt on the front zipper of her shorts. When he lifted his gaze to her face, she could see the hunger.

She pulled her gaze away, ignoring her rapidly beating heart. For years her only purpose in going to a party had been to pick up men. Not tonight.

Paula rested her hand on Sam's arm. "Whatever you want to do is fine with me."

The gesture was a little too familiar for Marcee's liking, but she grit her teeth and remained silent.

"Let's sit." Sam placed his paper plate on the table then shifted his gaze between Paula and Marcee. "Can I get you ladies something to eat? Or drink?"

"I'll take a beer," Marcee said.

"Iced tea for me, please," Paula said with a Stepfordworthy smile.

"Don't go anywhere." Sam's gaze remained focused on Marcee for an extra heartbeat.

Though Marcee told herself it didn't matter, a rush of pleasure washed over her.

"How long have you lived in Ellwood, Paula?" Marcee asked politely once they sat down.

"My husband and I moved here four years ago." Paula's smile widened, as if pleased by Marcee's sudden interest. "He was from Ellwood and had always wanted to come back. Thought it was the best place to raise kids."

The tension in Marcee's shoulders eased. Though it was none of her business who Sam hung around with, she found herself relieved to hear the woman had a husband. One who was apparently from Ellwood. "What's your husband's name?"

"Jake Dees," Paula said. "Most people from here called him J.J. He died in a car accident the year after we moved back."

So she wasn't married. She was a widow. Marcee pushed aside her disappointment and focused on the name. *J.J. Dees.*

An image of a tall boy with a shock of blond hair and a big toothy smile flashed before Marcee.

"I'm sorry for your loss," Marcee murmured, remembering a boy who always seemed in high spirits. "I remember J.J. He was a good guy."

"Thank you," Paula said simply. "He was my life."

When tears filled the woman's eyes, Marcee found herself blinking moisture away from her own. What would it be like to love a man that much? For a second her gaze strayed to the drink line where Sam stood patiently waiting. What would it be like if that person loved you back with equal intensity?

"You did say you were from Ellwood," Paula said, her words pulling Marcee back to the conversation. "Did you know my husband well?"

"Not really," Marcee said. "He was older. I remember him mostly from a store where I used to hang out. He worked the counter after school and in the summer. The thing I remember most about J.J. was his smile."

Paula smoothed back a strand of hair that the breeze had dislodged, the gesture as graceful and elegant as the woman herself. "That was my Jake."

The two women shared a smile, and Marcee realized that she was beginning to enjoy the evening.

"What brought you back to Ellwood?" Paula asked, appearing sincerely interested.

"My mother moved away with her new husband," Marcee said. "I came back to stay with my brother so he could finish high school in Ellwood."

"It's nice you were able to help out," Paula said. "Is your husband here with you?"

"I'm not married," Marcee said. "I guess I never found the right man."

She resisted the urge to glance in Sam's direction.

"He's out there," Paula said. "When I met Jake, I wasn't even looking, but the minute I met him, I knew he was something special."

An image of Sam taking time to console a crying child at the wedding flashed before Marcee. Not many men would have even given the boy a second glance.

"Why is it any time I interrupt two women, they're always talking about men?" Iris joked, sliding in beside Marcee on the picnic bench. "C'mon, you two. Surely you can find something more interesting to talk about?"

Marcee chuckled and turned to Iris. "I wondered where you were. I thought if she invited me then didn't bother to show—"

"You know I'd never do that to you. Unless," Iris's blue eyes twinkled, "Denzel Washington walked into my shop and begged me to run away with him."

Marcee couldn't help but laugh. "If that happened, I'd help you pack."

"Me, too," Paula added.

"Iris," Marcee said. "Do you know Paula Dees?"

"Of course," Iris said. "Tall cappuccino wet. I

think we were also in a spinning class together at the Y last year."

Paula heaved a sigh. "I need to get back there one of these days."

"Me, too," Iris said. "Hey, I've got an idea. How about the three of us take a class together? It'll give us some solid girl time."

"I'm up for it," Paula said. "But I work until four so it would have to be after that."

The two women shifted their gaze to Marcee. What could she do but agree? "Sounds good."

"It's a plan." Iris slid out from the picnic bench. "I hate to leave but I'm on the hospitality committee and they're making me work. I have to get more soda to put in the coolers."

Once Iris left, Marcee and Paula resumed talking as if there had been no interruption. Though Marcee didn't know Paula, the conversation never lagged. Soon Sam returned; a beer in one hand, an iced tea in the other.

"Did you know this gorgeous neighbor of yours is a CPA?" Paula asked as Sam passed out the drinks.

"I did know that," Sam said, taking a seat next to Paula.

Marcee wrapped her fingers around the icy can

and, though she told herself it was none of her business, she found herself wondering what was going on between Sam and the blonde. He'd sat next to Paula yet hadn't touched her since Marcee had seen them walking arm in arm earlier. Anyone watching them now wouldn't even think they were a couple.

"I don't want you to take this wrong." Paula's brows pulled together in a little frown. "You just don't look like an accountant to me."

"Okay, I'll bite," Marcee said with a smile, knowing what was coming. "What does an accountant look like?"

Paula paused and brought a finger to her lips. "Dark suit. No-nonsense expression. Pocket protector."

"Bingo." The dimple flashed in Sam's cheek and he shot Marcee a wink. "She's got you pegged."

Without thinking, Marcee stuck out her tongue, and they all laughed.

"Seriously, how did you pick that profession?" Paula asked, her eyes wide with interest.

"I've always liked math." Marcee's lips curved in a smile. "There was order and structure, and when you put it all together, it added up."

She realized with a start that the order and certainty found in mathematics was the complete opposite of what her home life had been like during that tumultuous time. Back then nothing had added up. No matter what she'd done, it had been wrong. "Being able to tie something up in a neat little package turns me on."

Just for fun she added a husky suggestiveness to her tone and watched the heat flare in Sam's eyes.

Paula didn't seem to notice. Her expression brightened as if she'd finally found the common ground she'd been seeking. "Baking is *my* passion."

The beer Marcee had just sipped took a wrong turn. She choked, but recovered quickly. "We all need passion in our lives."

"My wife liked to bake." Sam's eyes took on a faraway look. "Cakes, pies, you name it, Laura made it."

With scarcely contained eagerness, Paula shifted her attention to Sam. "What kind of pie is your favorite?"

Marcee stared down at the almost full can of beer. She'd only taken two sips, so she couldn't be drunk. But was she really at a barbecue on a Saturday night talking about *pies*?

Sam didn't hesitate. "Sour cream apple."

"I'll make it for you Thursday night," Paula said just as promptly.

Marcee went cold. Her gaze shifted between the two. They had another date planned? "I didn't realize the two of you were seeing each other."

"We aren't," Sam said, looking genuinely surprised. "Paula invited Fern and me over for dinner Thursday. Sort of a welcome-to-town kind of thing."

"Actually, Sam wants Fern to meet some nice kids before school starts in the fall," Paula confided. "My son Ted is very involved in school and we're hoping he'll introduce her around."

It was as if a knife had suddenly pierced Marcee's heart. Though she normally adhered to an every-man-for-himself philosophy, this was her *brother* about to be dissed.

Her brother, who'd been so excited about the possibility that he'd see Fern at the party that he put on a clean T-shirt. Her brother, whose face grew animated just talking about Fern. Her brother, who was smart and funny and loyal . . .

"Not that Fern hasn't already met some nice kids," Sam hastened to add.

Marcee slipped out of the picnic bench and stood, trying to get a grip on her rioting emotions.

"If you two will excuse me, I see someone over there," she waved in the direction of a large group of women, "who I need to speak with."

"It was great meeting you," Paula said. "Once the Y schedule comes out, I'll give you a call. Or, if you're ever free for lunch, let me know."

"If there's ever anything you need," Sam said in a light tone, "you know where to find me."

Marcee acted as if she didn't hear his comment. Because if he thought she'd stoop so low as to continue to be friends with a man who didn't consider her brother's feelings, well, it just proved he didn't know her at all.

Sam watched Marcee cross the yard, her shoulders stiff as any soldier, her head held high. He knew the talk about finding Fern some new friends had upset her, but surely she could see his side . . .

"She's very pretty, don't you think?" Paula's comment pulled Sam back from his reverie. "And I normally don't even like red hair."

"Marcee is beautiful," Sam acknowledged. In his mind "pretty" didn't begin to describe her. And not like red hair? What kind of person didn't like red hair?

"I think she'll be a good friend."

For a second Sam wasn't sure he'd heard correctly. "What?"

"A friend," Paula repeated. "She and Iris and I are all going to get together. Won't that be fun?"

"That'll be nice," Sam said, not surprised to hear Marcee was making friends. "You should—"

"Neither of you *should* do anything but get off your keisters and join us at the horseshoe pit."

Sam turned at the sound of Ron's loud voice just as the deputy slapped him on the back. "We're having a couples' tournament and I've signed you up."

Couples' tournament? What was he talking about? He wasn't part of any *couple*.

But Paula had already jumped to her feet. "My father and I used to pitch a few horseshoes when I was a kid." Her eyes danced with excitement. "This is going to be so much fun."

Paula's gaze slid to Sam's face and her smile faded. "Of course we don't have to . . . I mean, I know a lot of younger guys aren't into horseshoes."

"Whaddaya talking about?" Ron blustered. "Everyone likes horseshoes."

Sam glanced down at the plate of food he hadn't had a chance to eat. When he lifted his gaze, he caught a glimpse of red hair in the distance. The evening hadn't gone at all as he'd planned. But that was no reason to ruin it for Paula.

Sam rose to his feet. "I'll give it a try."

Paula's smile was blinding, and when she grabbed his hand and happily chattered as they made their way to the horseshoe pit, he didn't have the heart to pull away. Besides, it was merely a friendly gesture, and anyone seeing them together would realize that.

Marcee hadn't gone far when she saw Ron approach the picnic table. She was congratulating herself on getting out of there just in time when she heard Ron loudly say the word couple. She turned back and saw him gesturing with his head toward the area by the horseshoe stakes where a large group of men and women stood waiting. Apparently, the citizens of Ellwood had found an acceptable partner for their new sheriff.

Then she saw Sam holding Paula's hand, and it was as if someone had taken one of those horseshoe stakes and jammed it straight into her heart. But she dug her fingernails into the palms of her hands, squared her shoulders and kept walking toward the large group of women milling together on the lawn.

Tonight wasn't about Sam, it was about her. And

she was going to have a good time if it killed her.

An hour and a half later she'd downed two hot dogs, had more potato salad than one should ever consume in one sitting, and drank enough iced tea to fill a pitcher. She'd reconnected with some friends from high school, met some new women, and generally had a nice evening. But her heeled sandals had worn blisters on both big toes, the bugs had made their presence known, and Sam McKelvey was still pitching horseshoes with Paula. It was time, Marcee decided, to find Cam and head home.

But she'd barely gotten five feet when a familiar voice called her name.

Marcee turned and smiled. "Jeff. When did you get here?"

Tall, dark, and handsome were three words that described Jeff Spence. Like Paula, he was dressed up for the occasion, while most in attendance had dressed down. Instead of jeans and a T-shirt, the young attorney wore khaki pants with perfect creases and a button-up shirt.

"Just got here," he said, flashing a warm smile. "And believe it or not, I've already been propositioned."

Marcee pulled her brows together. "By who?"

"Ron Densmore," Jeff said with a laugh. "One

of the couples in the horseshoe tournament had to leave early and we're talking their place."

"We?"

"You," Jeff said, pointing to her, "and me," he said, pointing at his chest.

"I don't play horseshoes," Marcee said, but even before the words left her mouth, Jeff took her hand and pulled her toward the pits.

"The word isn't 'play,' it's 'pitch,'" he explained. "And it doesn't matter if you're good or not. The purpose is to have fun."

Too late Marcee realized the problem. Jeff thought she'd didn't want to play—er, pitch— because she wasn't any good. But the real reason was . . . well . . . come to think of it, she didn't have a reason.

"Okay," she said. "I'll give it a try."

After all, she'd told herself to venture outside her comfort zone and try new things. Now was one of those times.

Jeff slipped an arm companionably around her shoulders and gave a little squeeze. "I knew you'd be a good sport."

His arm was still there when they reached the horseshoe pits. When she saw who they were paired with, Marcee almost laughed. Who said God had no sense of humor?

Sam looked shocked. His gaze narrowed at the sight of Jeff's hand on her shoulder, and Marcee felt a sudden urge to explain. But she pressed her lips together and the desire quickly passed. After all, he hadn't felt the need to explain why he'd been walking arm in arm with Paula earlier.

Paula was elated when Jeff announced he'd found his partner and they were ready to play. After the introductions were completed, the match began. It didn't take long before it was apparent that Jeff and Paula were in a league of their own.

"If they were on the same team, they'd win it all," Marcee whispered to Sam when Paula followed Jeff's ringer by neatly wrapping her own horseshoe around the stake.

Paula squealed and clapped her hands, and Jeff gave her a congratulatory hug. For the last fifteen minutes they'd been their own mutual admiration society, while she and Sam had stood by and watched.

"I've never seen two people get so excited over a game of horseshoes," Sam said, shaking his head.

"I've never seen anyone pitch horseshoes in a skirt," Marcee said, shifting an admiring gaze to Paula. But her eyes widened in alarm when the blonde suddenly cried out and fell to the ground.

Marcee ran to Paula's side, Sam at her heels. "What happened? What's wrong?"

"I don't know." Jeff stood bent over Paula, his brow furrowed in concern. "One minute she was fine, the next she was on the ground."

The epitome of calm, Sam squatted down next to Paula and took her hand. "Tell me what happened."

"Putting that first responder training to good use," Jeff said, sounding peevish.

Marcee shifted her gaze back to Sam and felt a ping at the sight of him once again holding Paula's hand . . . until she realized that he was merely taking her pulse.

"My knee went out." Paula grimaced. "It's from an old injury. This happens every couple months."

Marcee pulled out her cell phone. "Do you want me to call the rescue squad?"

"No," Paula snapped, then softened the word with a smile. "I'll be fine. I just need to go home and ice it."

By now a crowd had gathered, and though Paula put on a brave face, Marcee sensed her embarrassment and wished there was something she could do to help.

"What the hell is going on here?" Ron pushed his way through the crowd, then stopped and cast Sam a questioning look.

"It's okay," Sam said. "Everything is under control."

"Then what is everybody gawkin' at?" Ron bellowed, the worry leaving his brow. "Haven't you seen a woman sittin' down before?"

The onlookers scattered, the conversational buzz loud.

"If you could just get me to my house, I'll be fine." Paula focused her gaze on Sam and a pleading look filled her eyes.

"Of course," he said without hesitation.

"I'm afraid you'll have to carry me," she said with an apologetic smile.

Jeff stepped forward. "I can help."

"Thanks," Sam said, looking puzzled at the offer. "But she's not that heavy."

Marcee was proud of Sam for stepping up to the plate and helping a woman in distress. But when Paula's arms circled his neck and her cheek pressed against his muscular chest, she found herself wishing it was Jeff who held the blond beauty in his arms, not Sam.

"She didn't say good-bye," Jeff said, his gaze firmly fixed on Sam's back.

"Sam didn't, either," Marcee said with a sigh, wondering how long he'd be gone. "Do you have any idea how far away she lives?"

"That's her place there." Jeff gestured to a sprawling brick ranch at the top of the hill. "'I wanted to help," he repeated, and Marcee realized she wasn't the only one who hadn't liked seeing Paula in Sam's arms.

From where she stood, Marcee heard Paula laugh. "Looks like the sheriff has the situation under control."

Jeff's lips pressed together. "Do you know if they're serious?"

Marcee blinked. "Who?"

"Sam and Paula," he said a trifle impatiently. "I got the impression they hadn't been dating all that long, but they're looking pretty cozy."

Sam's deep rumble of laughter mingled with Paula's, and the knot in the pit of Marcee's stomach turned to concrete.

"It hasn't been long," Marcee said. "But it looks like it's been long enough."

Marcee found Camden at the far end of the yard sitting on the ground, his back against a large oak, seemingly engrossed in a hand-held video game.

"Enjoying the barbecue?" she asked, stopping directly in front of him.

He looked up, and his green eyes—so like her own—gave little away. "This party sucks."

"Sounds like you're ready to leave."

Camden dropped the game into his pocket and scrambled to his feet. Marcee started walking up the large green expanse with Cam behind her. She'd talked to Jeff for about fifteen minutes, waiting for Sam to return. But it seemed that tending to Paula was a more time-consuming process than either she—or Jeff—had anticipated.

People waved or called out greetings as she and Cam walked up the large yard, but Marcee didn't stop to speak to them.

"Saw Fern," Camden said, the terse words pulling Marcee from her own disturbing thoughts.

She slanted the boy a sideways glance, but his gaze remained focused straight ahead. "What's new with her?"

"Not much," he said. "She and Sarah Beth Williams were hanging out."

So she had no time for you. Though Marcee hadn't been there, she instantly knew what had happened. Fern had blown Cam off in favor of her new, cool friend.

"That sucks," Marcee said when the silence lengthened.

"Yeah, well . . . " Camden lifted one shoulder in a slight shrug. "That's life, I guess."

"Still sucks." She could feel his gaze on her, but this time it was she who kept her gaze focused ahead.

"I saw you talking to her dad," Camden said.

"And his girlfriend," Marcee added.

"That's not his girlfriend," Cam said. "That's Mrs. Dees."

"I know who it is." Marcee kept her voice evenly modulated. "And I know for a fact they're dating. He's going to her house for dinner Thursday night. She's making him a sour cream apple pie."

Marcee wasn't sure why she'd added the last bit of information except that she had no idea how to even make a regular apple pie much less a sour cream one.

"Great." Cam stopped walking and slapped a hand against his leg, his face turning as red as his hair. "That is just freakin' great."

Marcee stopped, too, and lifted a brow. "Problem?"

"Her son Ted will be a senior, too." Cam's green eyes flashed. "Just like me. Just like Fern. If her dad and his mom are dating, that means Fern is probably going to end up spending time with Ted."

Marcee knew there was no *probably* about it, but saw no need to go down that road. "If she likes you, it won't matter how much she's around him. She'll—"

"You don't have any idea what it's like living in this town." Cam's voice grew louder and his tone more belligerent as he spoke. "In Ellwood, jocks rule. Anyway, Tom says you've never been able to keep a guy, so I don't think you're one to give advice."

Marcee's blood froze as the words slapped her in the face. She knew it was only Cam's frustration talking but it didn't make the comment any less harsh. "What else did wise ol' Tom tell you?"

"Nothing." Cam swept his hand in a sharp dismissive gesture. "Forget it. The point is nobody wants either of us."

Marcee opened her mouth to speak but no words came out. When Cam resumed walking, she found herself automatically following, Cam's words playing over and over in her head. *Nobody wants either of us.*

By the time they reached the car, she was angry. Angry at Sam for having a girlfriend. Angry at her brother for taking his sucky day out on her. And most of all angry at herself for caring.

She slid behind the wheel and closed the door . . . hard. Although Cam stood next to the car, he made no move to get in. Marcee rolled down the window on the passenger side. "Get in," she said.

Surprisingly, Cam opened the door and plopped into the seat. Marcee waited until he buckled his seat belt before she put the car in gear and pulled away from the curb, gravel spraying.

A thick blanket of tension filled the car, and she slanted a sideways glance at him. She half expected him to pull out the video game, but instead he sat, arms crossed, staring with unseeing eyes straight ahead. Despite his piercing and scraggly tuft of chin hair, he looked more like a sad and forlorn boy than an angry, belligerent young man. Shaggy without his Scooby Doo.

The thought bought the smile back to her lips. While she wanted nothing more than to ignore the little shit all the way home, old memories tugged at her. She remembered all too well the pain of being seventeen and feeling as if no one cared. In her case, no one *had* cared. But Cam . . . well, Cam had her.

Marcie broke the silence when she turned onto the street that led to their house. "You're wrong, you know," she said.

"About what?" Although his tone was defiant, the lost look in his eyes told her she'd made the right decision in taking the high road.

"About no one wanting either of us," she said matter-of-factly. "Because you have me."

"Yeah," Cam scoffed. "Once something better rolls around, you'll be long gone."

"I'm not going anywhere." Her fingers tightened on the steering wheel, the words both a promise and a vow. "And even when you go away to college, if you ever need anything, all you'll have to do is call."

Cam stared at her for a long moment, searching her face, but for what, she wasn't certain. Still, something he saw must have convinced him she was sincere because the tightness around his mouth eased. "You really mean it."

She shot him a wink. "Us redheads have to stick together."

"You're crazy," Cam said with a chuckle.

"I've been told that on occasion." She could almost feel Cam's spirits lift, and amazingly she knew it was because of *her*. Satisfaction flowed through her veins like warm honey. She wondered if this was what it was like to be a parent. Making that extra effort to rise above your own petty emotions and inclinations in order to do what was best for a child.

"I was out of line," Cam said unexpectedly just as Marcee reached their driveway.

"What are you talking about?"

"I shouldn't have repeated what Tom said." Cam's eyes were dark and filled with regret.

"No harm. No foul." Marcee summoned a smile. "Probably true anyway."

"No," Cam said. "You just haven't found the right guy."

An image of Sam flashed before her, but Marcee let a shrug be her response.

She didn't know why she was so disappointed in Sam. Though he'd made it clear to her he wasn't interested in dating, she'd hoped they could be friends.

But she would not stand by and let Cam be hurt. And she wouldn't smile prettily and be Sam's friend while he dated other women. Marcee shoved the car into park. No, she was done with the good sheriff. And as any of her friends could attest, once she was done with a guy . . . he was history.

The sound of hail pelting the windowpane woke Marcee from a fitful sleep. Without opening her eyes, she pulled the thin quilt around her and snuggled deep into the pillow.

After leaving the picnic and returning home, Cam had grabbed his iPod and gone straight to his room. Marcee had opened a bottle of wine and powered up her laptop. She'd worked until midnight on a friend's taxes then headed to bed, trying not to think where Sam and Paula might be right now . . . and what they might be doing. Thankfully, the wine relaxed her and she fell asleep immediately.

The ping of hail sounded from the window again and Marcee groaned. Rolling out of bed, she swept her hair back from her face and stumbled to the second-story window that overlooked the back-yard. Hopefully, pulling the curtains shut would muffle the irritating sound. But to her surprise the night sky was clear and a full moon shone brightly. Not a storm cloud in sight.

Before she could process the inconsistency, a spray of . . . rocks . . . hit the window. Suddenly she understood. She'd had a couple boyfriends in high school who used that trick to get her attention late at night. That had been fifteen years ago. It was hard to believe Camden's friends had not only mistaken her bedroom for his but used such a low tech way of contacting him. If they wanted her brother to come out and play, they should have just called him on his cell phone or sent him a text message.

Marcee jerked open the window and leaned out. "Haven't you ever heard of a cell—"

The words stuck in her throat when she saw a man—not a boy—standing in her yard, a handful of pebbles in one hand.

"You have your phone off," Sam said with a smile.

She started to return his smile until she recalled

seeing him walk across Ron's yard with Paula in his arms.

"Get out of my yard or I'll call the sheriff. I mean, I'll call the deputy."

Unfortunately, her tone lacked any real oomph, and consequently Sam's smile widened. "Good evening to you, too."

Marcee steeled herself against the blatant charm wafting up on the night breeze. "What do you want?"

This time her tone came out irritable and abrupt.

But his smile never wavered. Obviously, for a former Chicago detective, irritable and abrupt were to-be-expected responses.

"Meet me at the back door." Mr. Confident didn't even wait for her answer. Before she could open her mouth, the determined cop was out of sight.

Marcee grabbed the silky robe that matched her emerald green chemise. Leaving her feet bare, she hurried down the stairs. The minute she entered the kitchen, she saw Sam through the glass in the door. He wore the same jeans and shirt he'd had on earlier. She didn't need a detective's badge to realize he hadn't been home yet.

She glanced at the clock over the stove. He'd left the party with Paula hours ago. She wondered how he'd spent the rest of the evening. *Probably tucking Paula into bed . . .*

Pressing her lips together, Marcee flipped the dead bolt and jerked the door open. But when Sam moved forward as if to come inside, she stepped in front of him, blocking his path. "You can say whatever you want from there."

"It's cold out here." Sam wrapped his arms around himself and pretended to shiver. "Do you want me to freeze?"

Warm air fueled by a south breeze wafted in through the open door. It was a mild seventy degrees. A Mexican hairless couldn't freeze in this weather.

She should just tell him to leave, she thought. But when she opened her mouth, nothing came out. She'd walked away from more men than she could count. It had always been easy. Jenny once joked that she had a band of steel around her heart.

At the time, Marcee had appreciated the compliment. She'd taken pride in the fact that her heart could not be broken. Now there was a chink in her armor. And its name was Sam. Just standing this close to him stirred all sorts of emotions.

"Invite me in." His gaze dropped and desire flared in his eyes.

Marcee glanced down and realized the front of her robe had come open. She supposed she should be flattered that he'd thought of her. Instead all she felt was disappointment. She lifted her chin. "I'm not sleeping with you."

Something akin to shock flashed in Sam's eyes. "Do you really think that's why I'm here?"

Marcee jerked her robe closed and crossed her arms across her chest. "Why else would you have waited until one o'clock to come over?"

"Maybe because Fern just fell asleep." Sam brushed past her.

"Hey," Marcee said. "Where do you think you're going?"

Sam stopped at the kitchen table, rested a hand on the chair and turned. "Why are you so upset with me?"

Marcee wished she could tell him, but she didn't understand it herself. Part of it had to do with Cam. But the other part had to do with Sam and her feelings for him. In the past if she'd seen a man she'd once slept with hanging out with another woman, she would have just found herself another guy. No anger. No recriminations. Certainly no hurt.

The fact that she was even thinking of telling him her worries was a major red flag. "I'm not upset. I'm tired and I'm going back to bed. Good night, Sam."

Marcee turned on her heel and left him standing in the kitchen, expecting him to leave the same way he'd come in. Instead he followed her into the hall.

"Don't you even want to know how Paula is?"

"How's Paula?"

"When I left her she had her knee iced and her youngest was getting her some Advil."

"Good to know." Marcee lifted her chin. "Don't you want to know how Jeff is?"

His smile faded. "How's Jeff?

"I don't know," Marcee said. "I left the party with Cam."

The smile returned. "Good to know."

Marcee stared at him. Sometimes he really was the most infuriating man. "Now will you leave?"

"Not until you tell me what I did to upset you," he said.

How could she explain something she didn't understand herself? She knew the way she was feeling wasn't firmly grounded in reality, yet she couldn't seem to stop herself.

He took a step closer and captured her hand. "Please."

The feel of his skin against hers sent a disturbing rush of heat racing through Marcee's body. She jerked her hand back.

"You told me that Fern was your priority for this next year," she said, trying to rein in her emotions, which wasn't easy considering how close he was standing. "Yet, now you're dating Paula?"

"Is that what this is about?" Sam gave a little laugh, a note of disbelief in his voice. "You're jealous of *Paula*?"

Maybe it was the laugh. Maybe she was more tired than she thought. Or maybe he was . . . right. Whatever the reason, without considering that her next action would bring her dangerously close to the man inspiring such intense feelings, Marcee grabbed the front of Sam's shirt with both hands and pulled him to her.

"I told you what this is about." Her fingers tightened on the fabric. "You lied to me."

She now stood so close she could see the tiny flecks of gold in his eyes, smell the spicy scent of his aftershave and feel the waves of testosterone rolling off his body. The overwhelming sense of attraction that slammed into her underscored her susceptibility to his charm.

Instead of answering, Sam's arms unexpectedly slid around her waist. He leaned his head forward, resting against her forehead for a moment.

"I've never lied to you," he said in a low voice.

"You *did*." Marcee pushed him back, but he didn't let her go. If anything, his hold tightened.

"Listen." He met her gaze, his voice firm. "Fern *is* my priority. As for Paula, I didn't even know her until Ron introduced us."

Marcee hesitated. She hated herself for wanting to believe, for giving him a chance to explain instead of just walking away. "You were walking arm in arm, looking pretty cozy when I saw you."

The moment the words left her lips she cringed. Dear God, she did sound jealous.

"You've got it all wrong, Red." Sam lifted his hands and placed them on her shoulders. His hazel eyes locked on hers. "She took my arm, just like later she grabbed my hand. Though I don't know her well, I think she's just like that—you know, into that touchy-feely stuff."

Marcee resisted the urge to smile at the disgust in his voice.

"As far as the Thursday night dinner goes, *she* invited *me*." His gaze searched hers. "She thought it would be good for Fern to meet some more kids—"

"Some *nice* kids," Marcee reminded him, emphasizing the distinction. Her anger returned. "Because you don't want her associating with Cam—"

"Because I don't want Camden to be her *only* friend." Sam's tone turned soft and reassuring. "The more friends Fern has when school starts, the easier her transition will be."

Marcee had to admit what he said made sense. Still, she knew he didn't like Cam, had never liked him. "But if you had your choice, she wouldn't be friends with my brother at all."

Sam remained silent for a long moment. He dropped his hands from Marcee's shoulders. "I don't want them getting too close. You and I both know how strong those feelings can be . . . how hard to resist."

Marcee reluctantly nodded. Even now, as angry and hurt as she was with Sam, she still felt the pull.

"What else?" Sam took a step forward and rubbed his hands down her back. "Something is still bothering you."

He saw way too much, Marcee thought. Why couldn't he be like most guys—oblivious to everything but their own needs? But then, if he was like that, she wouldn't be so attracted to him. Determined to put some distance between them, Marcee moved to the sofa. She took a seat at the far end, sliding one leg beneath her. "Why did you come to see me now, in the middle of the night?"

Instead of remaining standing or taking a seat in the overstuffed chair across from the sofa, Sam plopped down next to her. If having him so close wasn't stressful enough, before she could sputter a protest he slipped an arm around her shoulders. "I've missed you," he said simply. "I can't explain it. I just needed to see you."

His words were like a soothing balm, and though she told herself not to read too much into them, she couldn't help but do just that.

"I wanted to see you," he repeated. "I care about you, Red."

To Marcee's horror, tears filled her eyes. Until two months ago she'd rarely cried. Then her doctor changed her birth control prescription. Ever since then she'd found herself sniffling at commercials and dabbing her eyes during sappy television love scenes.

She wasn't sure what brought the emotions rising to the surface now, unless it was the genuine caring in his eyes. She blinked rapidly but a few tears escaped and slid down her cheeks.

"Aw, Marcee." Sam raised his hands to her face and brushed the tears away with the pads of his thumbs. "I didn't mean to make you cry."

She drew a shuddering breath even as a couple more tears slipped past her lids.

Sam leaned close, and this time it wasn't his thumbs that brushed away the tears, it was his lips. "Don't cry, honey. Please don't cry."

He scattered kisses across her face and down her neck, and a warmth spread throughout her body. Oh, how she'd missed this intimacy.

She looped an arm around his neck and the green bracelet on her wrist caught her eye. She didn't need to read the embedded print to know what it said.

Reach High.

The words ran through her mind as Sam continued to kiss her. Would she be turning her back on all she'd achieved, negating all the strides she'd made, if she slept with Sam?

"Anyone ever tell you what a wonderful, strong woman you are?" he murmured against her neck.

Marcee arched her neck back, reveling in the closeness. "Hear it all the time . . . not."

"Well, you should, because it's the truth," he said, nibbling on her ear.

In that moment Marcee knew that tonight she and Sam would make love. She wouldn't be settling for anything or letting herself be used. She would be reaching high, opening her heart to the man she loved.

Loved?

She lifted her eyes and met his gaze, realizing with sudden wonder that it was true. She loved Sam McKelvey.

Marcee laid her head against his chest, inhaling the spicy scent of his cologne as she listened to his heart beating strong and hard against her ear. "I want to be close to you again, Sam. Like we were in the hotel room."

"I want that, too," he said, gently stroking her hair.

A warmth began in Marcee's heart and traveled all the way to the tips of her toes. The rightness of the decision she'd made moments before washed over her. She slid her hands up his sides, feeling his muscles tighten beneath her fingers.

"What about Camden?" Sam asked. He opened his mouth as if to say more then shut it without speaking.

"I checked on him earlier," she said softly. "You could explode a bomb in this house and he wouldn't wake up."

"Fern is the same way once she falls asleep."

Sam was still speaking when Marcee started unbuttoning his shirt. The buttons popped open easily beneath her fingers, but when she saw the white cotton beneath, disappointment sluiced through her. Marcee frowned and pulled impatiently at the T-shirt, tugging it loose from the waistband of his jeans.

"It's a disappearing shirt," Sam said with a wink. "Now you see it . . ." In a matter of seconds both the shirt and T-shirt lay on the floor. " . . . now you don't."

"A magician." Marcee skimmed her hands across the smooth flesh of his chest. "What other tricks do you have up your sleeve?"

A slow easy smile lifted the corners of Sam's lips. "How long do I have?"

Marcee smiled. "All night."

13

Sam leaned close, bracing a hand on the cushion beside her head. The position caused his chest to press against her full, generous breasts and he found himself wishing they were both naked. But he refused to rush.

Her fingers slipped through the hair at the nape of his neck and she drew his head down to hers. A wave of heat washed over him, gaining momentum at the desire simmering in her gaze. He kissed her gently but firmly, wanting her to know this wasn't going to end anytime soon.

Her lips opened, giving him access to the velvet heat of her mouth. His tongue fenced with hers, a slow, delicious thrust and slide that sent arrows of desire shooting straight to his groin. He'd never known such passion. Laura had always been so restrained, so concerned with propriety . . . both in and out of the bedroom.

Marcee . . . well, he doubted Marcee even knew the meaning of the word *restraint*. She had so much enthusiasm for life. When he was with her, everything seemed possible.

"This," he said, touching the silky green fabric, "has to go."

"You're the magician. Make it disappear." Even as she taunted him, Marcee slid her fingers across his chest, brushing the small bud of his nipple with the tip of her finger.

His body jolted and his hand tightened over hers.

Sam closed his eyes for a second, fighting for self-control. He wanted tonight to be special, not over in sixty seconds. Taking a deep steadying breath, he rose to his feet and pulled her up with him. "Close your eyes and count to ten. By the time you open them your clothes will be gone."

A suspicious look crossed her face. Sam brushed the hair back from her face with the edge of one hand and planted a gentle kiss on the exposed temple. "Trust me, sweetheart."

The suspicion faded and something warmer and more intimate took its place. Without further prompting, her lids lowered.

Ignoring the hunger tearing at the threads of his control, Sam placed a hand under the silky fabric and pushed it from her shoulders. Marcee continued to count, and just as she reached ten and opened her eyes, the last of the silky fabric dropped to the carpet.

Sam stood there for a long moment, awed by her beauty. "Good thing I'm not a real magician."

"Why is that?" Marcee asked, her voice low and husky.

He rested his hands on her shoulders. "Because the women in the audience would probably insist that I wave a wand and make your clothes reappear."

Marcee smiled, her hand absently skimming her belly and drawing his attention downward. Sam followed the direction of her hand, past the full perfect breasts, past the taut smooth skin of her abdomen to the thick thatch of curls . . .

Slow, he reminded himself, *take it slow.* His hands remained on her shoulders while his thumbs caressed the sensitive skin just above the swell of her breast. "You are so beautiful you take my breath away."

The light touch left sparks of electricity in its wake, but it was his words and the look in his eye that caused her blood to boil. She lifted her face to his. "Thank you for coming over."

"You're very welcome." He gave her a swift hard kiss. One that sent a shiver from her lips all the way to the tips of her toes.

She was still reeling when his belt and pants joined the rest of the clothes on the floor.

He nudged her back to the sofa. She could feel the heat from his body, and anticipation coursed up her spine at the fire in his eyes. She expected him to sit next to her, to take her in his arms, to lavish her face with kisses. Instead he knelt before her, resting his hands on her legs. "I want to make you happy."

"You do make—" She gasped as he pressed an open-mouthed kiss to her inner thigh. He looked up, and she saw the question in the smoldering depths of his eyes. In answer she opened her legs to him.

His mouth and tongue returned to the sensitive skin of her inner thigh, licking, biting, and kissing. Sensations more intense than any she'd ever experienced rose and swelled with each kiss, each flick of his tongue. Marcee brushed the flat of her hand across her now hypersensitive nipples just as Sam reached his destination and parted her. She cried out and came up off the sofa.

"Shh," Sam whispered. "Wouldn't want to wake the dead."

Her whole being was so focused on the overwhelming tension gripping her that for a second she wasn't sure what he meant. Until she remembered Camden, upstairs sleeping. She closed her eyes and moaned deep to herself. But when he put his tongue to her, working in and out as gently and expertly as a maestro would finger the strings of a Stradivarius, her control began to unravel.

With each touch, with each stroke, the fire inside burned hotter, until she hit the peak and exploded. She clamped her legs around him as waves of pleasure washed over her.

She had to cry out but the sound barely left her lips when Sam moved up on her, his mouth closing over hers, absorbing the cries. The change in position brought his erection front and center over her still pulsating spot. As they kissed, he rocked gently against her and her body heated up before it had even begun to cool.

Giving her another quick kiss, he grabbed his pants from the floor. Pulling out a small foil square from the back pocket, he opened the packet. In a matter of seconds the condom was in place and he was inside her.

But the angle was all wrong. He must have felt it, too, because he wrapped his arms tightly around her and fell back, taking her with him to the floor, his body absorbing the brunt of the fall.

Marcee ended up on top, a position that suited her just fine. She wrapped her hands around his wrist and pushed his hands over his head.

He didn't protest, merely gazed up at her with those sexy whiskey-colored eyes.

"I'm making a citizen's arrest," Marcee said. "Sam McKelvey, you are in my custody and under my control."

His eyes darkened, and though his expression remained serious, the dimple in his cheek flashed. "I'm a law-abiding citizen."

"That's a problem." Marcee straddled his hips and wiggled, feeling his hard length grow even more inside her. " 'Cause right now I'm looking for naughty."

Sam pulled his hands from her grasp, but before she could protest, he'd put them on her waist, guiding her movements, his hips rising to meet hers, driving home. "Call this a problem?"

"No. No. Oh no." Her head swam, assaulted by

the spicy scent of his cologne, the feel of his lips and the warm glide of his hands against her skin.

"Ah, Red, you feel so good," he moaned.

She sat back, reveling in the perfect rhythm she found with this man, loving the feel of him inside her. For a moment she felt as if she could go on like this all night . . . until Sam took a nipple in his mouth. Intense pleasure shot straight to her inner core, and without warning she shattered in the arms of the man she loved.

What sounded like a body hitting the floor woke Camden from a restless slumber. He'd been dreaming about Fern and Ted. Ted had been about to kiss Fern . . . and his fist had been about to connect with Ted's jaw, when he awoke with a jolt, his heart racing. Pushing himself up on his elbows, Cam listened for several minutes but there was only silence.

He laid his head back on the pillow and must have dozed off because when he awoke again it was to the sound of laughter. He glanced at the clock. Almost three. He thought about just pulling the pillow over his head but then began to second-guess himself. Had it been *laughter* he'd heard? Or *crying*?

Shit. He hated it when women cried. It made him feel so helpless. When his dad lived with them, his mom had shed buckets of tears.

Heaving a resigned sigh, Cam swung his legs over the side of the bed and stood. Clad only in cotton pajama pants and a T-shirt, he padded to his closed bedroom door. He stood there for a long moment, listening. While he heard sounds of movement, there was definitely no laughter or crying.

Still, he was already up. What would it hurt to check? Just take a few minutes to make sure Marcee was okay. He headed down the stairs and paused at the landing when he saw his sister. He started to call out a greeting, but pulled the words back when a guy stepped into view and he realized that Marcee wasn't alone.

Sam McKelvey wrapped his arms around Marcee when they reached the front door. When his hand cupped her bottom and he pulled her tight against him in an intimate gesture, Cam had little doubt what had been going on downstairs.

He clenched his hands together in tight fists. Marcee had said the sheriff was dating Mrs. Dees. If that was true, then what was Sam McKelvey doing here with her?

Standing in the shadows, Cam turned and headed silently back up the stairs. Marcee was a complicated person, but he knew she was a survivor. He only hoped that in this case his smart and beautiful sister knew what she was doing. Because as much as misery loved company, he didn't want to see them both screwed over by someone they cared about . . .

After Sam left, Marcee eased the door shut behind him and headed back upstairs, bypassing several squeaky steps. Though she knew Cam was a sound sleeper, she wasn't taking any chances.

She stopped off at the bathroom, hardly recognizing the woman staring back in the mirror. She tilted her head. Was this what love looked like? Shiny eyes and flushed cheeks? A smile that didn't want to leave her lips?

The knowledge that she was in love should have frightened her. After all, in thirty-two years this was a first for her. But the thought of loving Sam didn't bring with it fear, but rather a kind of wonder . . . that she was actually capable of giving her heart to someone.

Of course, she wouldn't be running out to buy a stack of bride magazines or pressing her face against any jewelry store windows to check out rings. No, she was realistic enough to know that she didn't live in some childhood fairy tale where you met, fell in love, and lived happily ever after. She lived in the real world where love often wasn't enough to guarantee a happy ending.

A lesser woman might have broken it off now, saving her heart the inevitable future pain. But Marcee had never been weak or fearful, or, for that matter, like other women.

As her friend Jenny had done before her, she would seize the day. And when it all fell apart, as she knew it would, she would survive.

She nodded to herself in the mirror, stripped off her clothes and hopped into the shower. She'd thought the soothing warmth of the water would relax her, but all it did was get her nerve endings jumping. The stream of water caressing her bare skin reminded her of the soft touch of Sam's hands. And when she slid the perfumed gel over intimate parts of her body, she remembered the heat, the passion, but most of all the gentleness.

Wrapping a towel around her still damp body, she grabbed her phone and headed to her room. Once there she flipped on the light and moved to the window.

Just as she'd sensed, Sam stood at *his* window staring out into the night.

She punched in his number and before it could ring once, he answered.

"I miss you," he said in greeting.

Though she'd planned to keep this casual and light, her heart swelled with emotion. "You left not thirty minutes ago."

"An eternity," he said in a deep sexy voice that sent blood coursing through her veins like an awakened river.

"Very smooth, Sheriff."

"I meant what I said earlier. I want nothing more than to sleep with you curled next to me and wake in the morning and have those beautiful green eyes be the first thing I see."

The image he painted was so vivid it made her heart ache with longing. She'd wanted that, too. But they had to be realistic. "This is Ellwood."

There was no need to say more.

"I know," he said with a sigh. "Not to mention we have two teenagers who are looking to us to set a good example."

Marcee wasn't sure about the veracity of that statement but she didn't argue. Certainly, Cam had been forced to endure his share of gossip about his mother's sex life. He shouldn't have to endure the same kind of remarks about his sister.

Thankfully, what was done in the privacy of one's own home was still private.

With one hand, Marcee loosened the towel wrapped around her. "Remember what I said to you about friends not letting friends see them naked?"

"I do," Sam said, and despite the darkened expanse between them, Marcee swore she could see his eyes take on a devilish gleam.

"I still believe that, but you're not just my friend, you're my *special* friend." She flicked her wrist and the towel fell to the floor.

She heard Sam's quick intake of breath as she stepped to the window and stood there illuminated in the light. After a moment she stretched, leaned forward, and blew him a kiss. "Sweet dreams."

Before he could say a word, Marcee pulled down the shade and clicked off the phone. A satisfied smile hovered on the edge of her lips. At least now she wouldn't be the only one going to bed hungry for more.

Marcee stared at Cam across the breakfast table. Her little brother was definitely acting strange. When he'd come downstairs, he grunted as he made his way to the cupboard containing the Pop-Tarts. That was totally normal. What surprised her was that he was already out of bed at nine o'clock.

Not only that, he'd eschewed his normal grunge look for black jeans and a button-up shirt. His hair even looked freshly spiked. She watched him drop the pastry square into the toaster.

"You're up early." She took a sip of coffee, savoring the taste. She'd brewed it extra strong, just as she liked it. She could almost feel the caffeine jump-start her sluggish blood.

Cam stared at her for a long moment. There was a look, a challenge, in the boy's eyes that didn't make any sense. Marcee supposed she could ask what was on his mind, then decided if he had something to say to her, he'd say it. Instead she focused on the obvious. "Going somewhere?"

"Church," he told her.

The response was so unexpected that Marcee laughed. "Yeah, right. Where are you *really* going?"

"I told you."

Marcee narrowed her gaze. He didn't look like he was joking. Still, he had to be playing her. "What church?"

Clearly impatient, Cam retrieved the Pop-Tart before it had finished toasting and took a bite. "Ellwood Christian," he said around a mouthful of the pastry.

Marcee paused. Shirleen had married Camden's dad at Ellwood Christian. If he actually was going to Sunday services, it made sense he'd attend that church.

"Let's assume for the sake of argument that I believe you," Marcee said. "I still don't understand why you're going."

"Why do most people go to church?" Cam plopped down in the chair opposite her, answering the question with one of his own.

Marcee took another sip of coffee. At times like this she realized how much more she had to learn about her little brother.

"Want to go?" He shoved the rest of the pastry into his mouth.

For a moment she was taken aback. Other than weddings, it had been years since she'd set foot in a church. "No thanks."

Cam chewed thoughtfully for several seconds. "You're scared," he said finally. "I never pegged you for a chicken."

Despite her head telling her that this was an obvious ploy to get her to change her mind and that she'd do best to just not respond, she found herself rising to the challenge in his tone. "I'm not afraid."

Resting his elbows on the table, Cam leaned forward. "Then come with me."

From the time Marcee had been a little girl, she'd had difficulty resisting a dare. But go to church? *The* gathering place for the whole community?

If you do what you've always done, you'll get what you've always gotten.

Marcee hesitated. She'd gone to the barbecue last night. She'd let Sam get close. No, two major events in one week were more than enough. She shook her head.

Something that looked a lot like disappointment skittered across Cam's freckled face. Then his lips lifted in a sly smile. "I knew you wouldn't do it," he taunted. "You act tough, but inside you're a weenie."

Marcee straightened in her seat and returned her cup to its saucer with a clatter. "I'm no weenie."

"Words," Cam scoffed. Her brother did a good job of hiding his emotions behind a brash exterior but she wasn't fooled.

She stared into those green eyes, so like her own, and looked beneath the surface. In the end it wasn't the challenge in the liquid depths that caused her to reconsider, it was the hint of vul- nerability. She wasn't sure why he wanted to go to church and wasn't sure that mattered. Walking in alone wouldn't be easy. Yet she had no doubt Cam was going to do it . . . with or without her.

"Okay," she said. "I'll go."

The look of pleasant surprise on his face brought

a smile to Marcee's face. Until she realized just what she'd agreed to do.

Sam stared out the truck windshield and stifled a yawn. When he left Marcee's house, it had been after three. By the time he fell asleep it was close to four. He'd tossed and turned, thinking about what happened and trying to make sense of it.

If pressed, he would have sworn he went to her house simply to talk. But there hadn't been much talking, he thought with a rueful smile. Not that he regretted making love to her. He would never regret the closeness they'd shared. When she was in his arms, his world was in perfect sync.

"Grateful Bread after church as usual?"

Fern's question pulled Sam from his reverie.

"Of course." Sam wheeled the truck into the church parking lot and turned off the ignition. He'd negotiated weekends off into his contract with the city, and lunch with Fern on Sunday quickly became a habit.

Though the Grateful Bread was primarily a bakery, it also served soup and sandwiches. Sam had developed an affinity for their pastrami on rye. Even more important, because most of the church attendees preferred the Coffee Pot in downtown Ellwood, he and Fern weren't usually disturbed.

His one-to-one time with his daughter had been the best thing to come out of moving to Ellwood. As for small town life itself . . . well, it had taken some adjustment. He wasn't sure he'd ever get used to the scrutiny. Still, the slower paced life-style had given him what he'd come here for—the opportunity to forge a stronger relationship with his daughter.

Fern pushed open the passenger door and jumped out. "C'mon, Dad."

Sam glanced at his watch. By his calculations the service wouldn't be starting for another ten minutes. Yet Fern acted as if they were already late.

"What's the rush?" Even as he spoke, he pushed open his door and stepped out of the truck.

"If we're late," Fern called over her shoulder to him as she started across the parking lot, "we'll have to sit in the front row again. Remember two weeks ago?"

Sam picked up his pace and fell into step beside her. Of course he remembered. He'd overslept and they arrived just before the opening prayers. The only seats available had been down front, within spitting distance of the pulpit.

Stuck in that very public location, Sam had felt

as if all eyes in the room were focused on him. He'd told himself that it wasn't so, but the following week enough people kidded him about being in the front row that he realized even if *all* eyes hadn't been on him, *most* were.

Thankfully, today when he entered the lobby of the church he could see that there were still a few seats available in the back.

Sam had his eyes so firmly fixed on the arched opening leading to the sanctuary that he didn't notice his neighbor, Mrs. Applebee, until she stepped in front of him.

"Why, Sheriff, I didn't expect to see *you* this morning." The decidedly curious gleam in her eye was a clear giveaway that the woman had something more than a simple greeting on her mind.

Dorothy Applebee was an even bigger gossip than his deputy, Ron. The look in her eyes, coupled with the fact that she was in the lobby rather than in front with the rest of the choir mates, made him uneasy. If he ended up in the front row again . . .

"We always come to the ten-thirty service," he heard Fern say.

"Yes, I know," Dorothy said. "But I heard you and your father were out pretty late last night."

"Not that late," Fern said.

Though Fern's tone was pleasant, Sam knew his

daughter well enough to sense—and share—her irritation.

This was the part of small town life he especially disliked. How late he stayed out shouldn't be anyone's business but his own. Still, he *was* a public servant.

Sam forced a polite smile. "I don't remember seeing you at the barbecue."

"I wasn't there." Dorothy waved a dismissive hand. "My lumbago was acting up. But I heard all about it."

Of course she had.

"I hope you're feeling better." Even as he spoke, Sam attempted to step around her. But she'd read his intentions perfectly and blocked him.

If she hadn't been close to seventy—and affected with lumbago—she'd have made a terrific noseguard in the NFL, he thought.

"I heard you and Paula are quite the couple." Behind her trifocals, Dorothy's eyes took on a dreamy look. "Sharing a picnic dinner, pitching horseshoes together, walking hand in hand—"

"Actually," Sam interrupted before she could continue, "last night was the first time I'd met Paula, er, Mrs. Dees."

"First or fiftieth," Dorothy said. "When the attraction is there, it's there."

"That's true," Sam said, thinking not about Paula, but Marcee. From the moment he'd seen the beautiful redhead at Jenny's wedding reception, he knew she was someone special.

"My oh my, you *are* smitten," the woman chortled. "I can't wait to—I mean I need to rejoin my choir mates."

Without another word she hurried off.

Fern chuckled. "Good one, Dad."

Sam stared open-mouthed at the retreating figure. "She completely misunderstood what I was saying."

Fern placed a comforting arm on his sleeve. "Hey, she heard what she wanted to hear."

"I'm not interested in Paula Dees as anything more than a friend," Sam said firmly, determined to make sure Fern understood.

Paula might be an intelligent, beautiful woman, but if he was interested in dating someone, it wouldn't be her. She was too much like his first wife. While he was glad he'd married Laura— because otherwise he wouldn't have Fern—their relationship had its share of problems.

"*I* know that," Fern said in a matter-of-fact tone. "And *you* know that. But face it, in this town it's more about the gossip than the truth."

The words sounded oddly familiar to him. Then

he remembered . . . it was almost word for word what Marcee had relayed about Ellwood and *her* experience.

Fern patted him on the shoulder. "You just have to do what you want and ignore what people say."

Sam pulled his brows together. He slanted a sideways glance at her. "It used to bother you."

"I know," Fern said. "But talking to Sarah Beth made me realize that trying to control what others think is a losing battle."

"Sarah Beth?"

"A girl at the barbecue," Fern said. "I thought she was nice. For a moment I thought I might have made a new friend."

The pain in Fern's voice was palpable, and Sam's heart went out to her. He knew how much his daughter wanted to make friends. "What happened?"

"When she asked who I'd been hanging out with, I mentioned that Cam and I had become good friends." Fern lifted her chin. "First she laughed like I'd said something funny. Then, when she realized I was serious, she started going on and on about Cam being a loser." Fern's voice grew tight. "I told her that wasn't true. He's in youth symphony and his science project from last year just won a major award. Besides that, Cam is cool. He's definitely got his own style. Sarah Beth didn't want to hear it."

Fern paused for breath, and Sam cast a longing glance at the couple of seats remaining in the back row. It took everything he had not to urge her forward. But if he had to sit up front again, he'd sit up front. Fern needed to get whatever was troubling her out, and he wanted to listen.

"You know what she wanted to talk about?" It must have been a rhetorical question because Fern continued without waiting for a response. "His hair. Then about a poem he'd once written for a girl he liked in eighth grade. According to Sarah Beth, this girl was way out of his league. Said they'd passed the poem around and all had a good laugh."

Fern's eyes grew dark. "I can't imagine how that must have hurt him."

Sam had heard that same story from Ron. It was every adolescent boy's nightmare. He'd been surprised that Ron found it so amusing. "I'm surprised she didn't bring up him not going out for basketball."

"It's *his* life," Fern said, her eyes flashing. "*His* choices. Not anyone else. I'm proud of him for being his own person. And I'm going to tell him so . . . if . . . if he'll speak to me."

"Did you two have a . . . " He paused, having

learned the need to tread lightly when a teenage girl's emotions were involved. " . . . disagreement?"

"Not exactly." Fern bit her lower lip. "Last night I'd just started talking to Sarah Beth when Cam wandered over. I blew him off. I don't know why, but I did."

"I've done things like that, too." Sam thought of Marcee and how he'd walked off with Paula last night without even saying good-bye to her. She hadn't made a big deal of it, but he was determined to make it up to her. "All I can do is try to make it right."

Fern's brows pulled together in puzzlement. "I mean," he said, "all *you* can do is try to make it right."

Fern set her jaw in a familiar determined tilt. "As soon as I get the chance, I'm going to do just that."

Sam looped an arm around her shoulder and in his mind echoed her vow. When he saw the two redheads sitting side by side in the second to the last pew, Sam knew this was not only Fern's chance to right a wrong, but his as well.

By the time the church service ended, Marcee
wished she'd started clucking and walked away
from Cam's challenge. She wasn't ready for this.
For fifteen years she'd done a good job of not
thinking about this town. But sitting in the pew
next to Camden had brought the memories flood-
ing back.

Memories of the time immediately after she'd
been kicked out of the house. Other than not
hearing her brother cry, she hadn't done anything
wrong. Yet people she'd known her whole life
played judge and jury and found her guilty.

Like in church. She could feel all eyes on her. It

was like one of those horrible dreams where she was walking down the street in her underwear and everyone was staring. She reminded herself this was the nature of small towns, but it didn't make her any more comfortable.

Thankfully, her brother seemed oblivious to the scrutiny. so she'd kept her mouth shut. She didn't want to ruin the morning for Cam, who seemed genuinely pleased to be in church and have her sitting beside him.

"How about we stop somewhere and get a latte?" she said, giving Ron and his cohorts in the lobby a dismissive glance as she and Cam made their way through the departing church crowd.

"How about you join us at Grateful Bread instead?"

Marcee stilled at the sound of the rich baritone. With her heart in her throat she turned and found Sam and Fern staring at her with hopeful smiles.

"Cam already ate." The inane comment didn't say much for her communication skills, and she swore Sam hid a smile.

"Iris makes a terrific apple streusel coffee cake." Fern took a step closer to the boy, her eyes taking on a pleading expression. "Cam loves sweets."

Though Fern's tentative smile had apology written all over it, Marcee knew the girl had hurt her brother last night, and she waited to see how Cam would respond.

Fern must have sensed that he was on the verge of saying no because she placed a hand on his arm. "I'd *really* like it if you came."

His gaze locked with Fern's, and something in his eyes must have reassured her because she slid her hand slowly down his arm until her fingers intertwined with his.

"Fern's right." Cam shifted his gaze to Marcee, the brooding look that had blanketed his face replaced with a calm, sure look. "I am hungry."

"What about you, Marcee?" Sam asked.

After last night, she wasn't sure how to act around Sam. Like a neighbor? Friend? Lover?

But like his daughter, Sam seemed to have a sixth sense. He stepped closer and his eyes urged her to come with him. Still she wavered.

Out of the corner of her eye Marcee saw Dorothy Applebee hurrying toward them, still dressed in her choir robe.

"Better decide quickly." Sam flashed a barely perceptible glance at the woman. "Torpedo approaching at nine o'clock."

The two teens exchanged puzzled glances but Marcee made the connection. Without giving herself a chance to consider the full ramifications of what she was about to do, she gestured toward the door. "Damn the torpedo. Full speed ahead."

On the way to the café Cam chatted easily. But when Marcee pulled her Saturn into the small lot next to the Grateful Bread, he turned silent and two lines of tension furrowed his brow. She couldn't help but wonder if he was having second thoughts.

Sam and Fern pulled into the parking spot next to their car and they all walked in together. The café was surprisingly crowded, but Sam spotted an empty table next to the bakery case.

Marcee took a seat in the chair Sam pulled out and inhaled deeply. "I love the way this place smells."

"Dad and I come here every week," Fern said. "The food is great."

Though Fern's smile was easy when she spoke to Marcee, it changed when she shifted her gaze to Camden.

Cam sat staring at the nearby bakery case as if he'd never seen freshly baked muffins before. The silence lengthened and Marcee searched her brain for a neutral topic.

She'd just discarded the weather as a viable option when the waitress stopped by to take their order. The server was another former classmate, and she and Marcee chatted for a few minutes about the menu, the weather, and Iris, who had kitchen duty today.

The minute the woman left, Cam broke his silence.

"I shouldn't have interrupted you last night," he said to Fern, his chin tilted up, his voice strong. "You were talking with Sarah Beth. It was rude of me to interrupt."

Marcee didn't know who was more surprised by the sincere sounding apology, her or Fern.

"Ohmygod, no." Fern reached over and covered Cam's hand with hers. "I'm the one who should apologize. Will you forgive me?"

"There's nothing to forgive." Cam's fingers curved around Fern's.

"No hard feelings?" Fern asked, an anxious look on her face.

"None," Cam said.

Marcee exhaled the breath she'd been holding. Why hadn't anyone warned her that being a parent—even a fill-in one—could be so stressful?

She shifted her gaze to Sam and found he'd taken over Cam's job of watching the bakery case.

The waitress brought the drinks. With a show of reluctance, Cam released Fern's hand.

Marcee experienced a twinge of envy. What would it be like to be so young and innocent again? She shrugged off the thought, reminding herself that both Fern and Cam still had a lot to learn about life and love.

"This place has been around forever." Marcee glanced around the café. "My mother used to stop here all the time for baked goods."

"They do a good take-out business." Sam gestured with his head toward the line forming at the bakery counter.

Marcee thought Cam might throw in some comment. After all, he was a lifelong Ellwood resident and probably very familiar with the café.

But Cam merely continued to stare into Fern's eyes.

"There was a place similar to this not far from my old apartment in Chicago," Marcee said. "I bought all my bread there."

"When my mother was alive, we never went to a bakery." Fern pulled her gaze from Cam. "Mom loved to bake. She used to make the best sourdough cinnamon rolls. Didn't she, Dad?"

Sam nodded.

"Sometimes if I close my eyes I can still smell them." As if to illustrate, Fern drew a deep breath.

But when she exhaled, tears filled her eyes.

Sam placed a reassuring hand on his daughter's arm but she seemed too lost in the memories to notice.

"Sounds like your mother was quite the home-maker," Marcee said softly.

Before Fern could answer, Paula Dees stopped at the table.

"Paula." Sam scrambled to his feet. "You're walking."

"A little ice and a lot of ibuprofen did the trick." She shifted her gaze to include Marcee. "I'm sorry I ruined the match. I hope Jeff understood . . . "

"We all understood," Marcee said with a re-assuring smile.

Sam glanced around the café. "Where are your sons?"

"Still in bed," Paula said with a little laugh. "We're planning to go to church this evening so I let them sleep. Anyway, I thought I'd stop in and grab a quick cup of coffee. Jake and I used to al-ways go out together after church. Even after all this time, Sunday mornings without him are still hard."

"Why don't you join us?" Sam heard Marcee say. "There's more than enough room."

Paula glanced around the table. "I don't want to intrude . . . "

"You're not," Marcee said, sounding surprisingly sincere. "Cam and I ran into Sam and Fern at church and he invited us to breakfast. I'm sure if you'd been standing there he'd have invited you, too."

Sam opened his mouth to protest. That wasn't how it had been. He'd asked Marcee because he wanted to spend time with her. But that admission was for another time and place. He turned and found Marcee staring at him with an expectant gaze. "I'll get another chair," he said.

Once Paula was seated, Sam made quick work of the introductions.

Marcee acted as if she'd asked a dear friend to join the group.

Cam scowled and turned silent.

Fern was clearly puzzled.

"Fern was just telling us how much her mother loved to bake," Marcee said once the waitress had taken Paula's order and refilled their coffees.

Sam resisted the urge to kick Marcee under the table. She'd seen Fern's response to that bittersweet memory. Surely she realized that was one topic best left alone.

"Your father mentioned that to me last night," Paula said to Fern, shooting a smile in Sam's direction. "Probably because I was going on and on about how much *I* love to bake. Did your mom have a favorite recipe?"

"Sourdough cinnamon rolls," Fern said politely.

"Mmm, I bet those *were* good," Paula said. "How did she make them?"

Perhaps it was the genuine interest in Paula's eyes that made the difference. Whatever the reason, this time there were no tears and Fern seemed eager to explain.

Sam listened in amazement. He'd known Fern and Laura were close but had never realized how much they'd done together. Hearing Fern describe in vivid detail some of their culinary catastrophes and successes over the years soon had him second guessing himself.

How could he hope to build that kind of relationship with her in one short year?

"My friend Jenny's mother is a fabulous cook," Marcee interjected when Fern stopped to take a breath. "But Jenny can barely boil water. Still, she and her mother are close."

Marcee shifted her gaze to Sam, and he realized with a start that she'd sensed his concern.

This was her way of telling him that he and Fern would be okay, even if they didn't share common interests.

"I like to think my boys and I have a good relationship even though I can't take them hunting and fishing like their father," Paula echoed. She shifted her gaze to Fern. "My husband was killed in a car accident four years ago."

"Out on the old highway," Cam said, speaking for the first time since Paula had sat down.

Paula shifted her gaze to Cam. "Did your sister tell you she went to school with him? Of course, Jake was a lot older."

"Twice in one day," a familiar voice twittered. "What are the odds?"

Dorothy Applebee and several of her choir mates stood tableside trying to look nonchalant but failing miserably.

Sam suppressed a groan. He and Fern had been coming to the Grateful Bread every week since they'd arrived in Ellwood. Why was it that the one Sunday he wanted some time with Marcee, everyone else in town showed up here as well?

"Dorothy, this is a surprise," Paula said, a warm note of welcome in her tone. "I thought you and the girls always went to the Coffee Pot on Sundays."

"We do . . . we did." Dorothy's rouged cheeks turned a deep pink. "But we thought we'd try someplace different for a change."

The older woman's gaze shifted between Sam and Paula. She nodded approvingly. "How nice to see you both together again."

The inference was clear to Sam, but the older woman had gotten it all wrong. He was here with Marcee, not Paula.

"You remember Marcee Robbens?" Sam asked. "And her brother, Camden Smith?"

"Of course." Dorothy's smile froze on her lips. "How is your mother and her latest hubby? What was his name? Crazy Dog?"

"Mad Dog," Cam said.

"Ah yes . . . Mad Dog." Dorothy wrinkled her nose. "I don't mean any disrespect, but what was the woman thinking?" She shifted her gaze to Marcee. "Of course, it was the same when you and that Fuller boy got carried away on the davenport while your little brother was upstairs crying. When a person lets hormones rule, no good comes of it."

Sam clenched his jaw. How dare the woman make such insinuations concerning something she knew nothing about. He opened his mouth to tell the old biddy just that but Marcee spoke first.

"It's been interesting coming back here after all these years," Marcee said smoothly, her eyes giving nothing away. "Do you know what I've discovered?"

"What is that, dear?" Dorothy asked.

"Nothing has changed."

The pickup hit a rut in the back road and Marcee placed a hand on the dash to steady herself. The area they were headed for appeared to be definitely off the beaten path.

"Sorry 'bout that." Sam shot her an apologetic smile. "Guess I need to keep my eyes off you and on the road."

Marcee stared at him through lowered lashes, accepting the compliment. When they stopped home after breakfast to change clothes, she'd been torn. Practicality said if they were going to hike she should put on long pants. Vanity insisted she wear the olive green shorts that showed off her legs to full advantage and the caramel colored cotton tee that emphasized her full breasts.

Vanity had won, of course. The only concession she'd made for practicality was to leave her flimsy sandals behind.

Sam had on a pair of worn jeans and a faded Chicago PD T-shirt. It should have been a crime, Marcee decided, for any man to look that sexy. And this afternoon, he was all hers.

She couldn't believe how things had turned around. When she'd left for church this morning, she had given up hope of a good day.

Then she'd run into Sam and the world started looking brighter. It took a nosedive when old Mrs. Applebee showed up but rebounded nicely when Cam asked Fern to go to the lake with him. When Sam called shortly after the kids had left and asked her to spend the afternoon with him, a wonderful day seemed guaranteed.

Alone with Sam, she could relax and be herself. Marcee exhaled a happy sigh, wondering when it had gotten so comfortable between them. She thought about it for a second and realized it had been this way from the beginning. From the moment she met him in that ballroom, she'd felt at ease, with no need for the usual nerves.

"You seem in an awfully good mood," Sam said.

"I love being outdoors." Marcee smiled. "In fact when I was a child, I dreamed of being a forest ranger."

"Yeah, right." Sam began to laugh but stopped almost immediately. "You're serious?"

She leaned back and let the sun shining through the truck windows caress her face. "I knew you wouldn't believe me."

"It's just that being a CPA and a forest ranger are so . . . different." He slanted a sideways glance as he steered the truck around another hole in the road.

"What can I say . . . I have weird tastes."

Sam looked askance.

When Marcee made the connection she giggled, the sound feeling odd in her throat. "Except for you, of course."

He chuckled and the sun seemed to shine even brighter. Marcee couldn't remember the last time she'd felt so carefree.

"Thanks for inviting me," she said. "I can't imagine anything better than an afternoon of hiking."

"I can think of one or two things," Sam said with a devilish wink.

Just for the hell of it, Marcee giggled again.

Sam turned off the highway onto a local road. "I'm surprised you're so into nature."

"Actually, I'm a physical activity junkie," Marcee said. "Skiing, snorkeling, hiking, I love it all. One of these days I plan to give rock climbing a try."

"Really? Rock climbing is something I've loved since I was a kid. My father was into it big-time."

"You're kidding me."

"Scouts honor." Sam raised three fingers. "Still have the gear in my closet."

The realization that they shared this interest took Marcee by surprise and pleased her, though she wasn't sure why. It wasn't as if they'd ever be scaling vertical walls together. "I've wanted to do it for years. Just never found the time."

"The YMCA has a climbing wall," Sam said. "It's not the same as being outdoors on a sheer rock face but it gives you a taste. You should give it a try."

"I just might do that." Marcee couldn't believe he was taking her dreams so seriously. "Do you go on many climbing trips?"

"When I was younger, I went on quite a few with my dad, but not so much since I married," he said. "I once suggested to Laura that we splurge on a trip to Mallorca, but she wasn't excited about the idea. She felt I put myself in danger every time I went to work and didn't see why I had to do it when I was off duty. Once I thought about it, I could see her point."

Most of the men she knew would have said to hell with a wife's fears and gone anyway. Or they'd have stayed home and held it against her. Not many would have understood . . .

Sam pulled off the road and into a graveled area while she was thinking about how unique he was. He shut off the ignition, released his seat belt, opened the door and stepped out of the truck.

After rounding the front of the pickup, he opened her door. When he reached out and took her hand, a familiar burst of electricity shot clear to her toes.

He must have felt it, too, because as she stepped down he pulled her to him, the faint spicy scent of his aftershave teasing her nostrils. Pushing the truck door shut with one hand, he pressed her body against the sun-warmed metal. "You know, I couldn't sleep last night."

Marcee widened her eyes in mock surprise. "Why not?"

He nuzzled her neck. "I had a certain redhead on my mind."

Her breath caught in her throat, but before she could say a word, he began kissing her. He kissed her on the lips, on the cheeks, on her neck. He kissed her until her knees grew weak. He kissed her until desire, hot and insistent, flowed like molten lava through her veins. But when she reached for his belt buckle, his fingers wrapped around hers.

"Later," he said in a strangled voice. "I brought you out here to hike. That's what we're going to do."

Marcee slid her fingers through his hair. "I don't mind . . . "

"But I do." He stepped back and the tightness of his jaw told her the effort it took. After a long moment he held out a hand. "Ready to hit the trail?"

Heaving a frustrated sigh, Marcee ignored his hand and started walking.

Sam wondered if he'd always been insane or if this was a relatively new phenomenon. What *sane* man would give up an opportunity to make out with a beautiful woman in order to *hike*?

But as much as he liked kissing Marcee, he didn't want her to think he'd brought her out here for a repeat of last night. Not that he wouldn't like to make love to her again, but he knew how much she'd looked forward to hiking.

"Did you say hike or meander?"

He glanced up to find Marcee standing about twenty-five feet in front of him. She began to saunter back, her laughing green eyes taunting him. "You're moving slow as a slug."

A slug? He'd set a new record for the fifty-yard dash when he was in the police academy. Now, he covered the distance between them in several long strides and then kept on going.

When he was a good distance ahead, he turned and danced from foot to foot like a boxer in a ring. "Who are you calling a slug?"

This time it was her turn to play catch-up. Once she reached him, they continued uphill, side by side, talking easily. When they reached a fork in the path, Sam turned to face her. "You know what I like about you? You're spunky."

"Know what I like about you?" she asked, gazing up at him through lowered lashes.

"What?"

"You're hunky."

Sam chuckled. *Definitely spunky.* "Well, hunky wants to know which way you want to go. Either way will take us where I want to go."

Marcee glanced at the fork in the road. "Left. Everyone goes right."

"Going against the grain again." Sam laughed. "Tell me, Ms. Robbens, have you always been the rebel?"

"Actually, in high school I was pretty much a straight arrow," she said in a surprisingly serious tone. "The funny thing was, all anyone saw was a pretty girl with big boobs and an even bigger mouth. I swear I was the only girl at Ellwood High who got a rep without sleeping with a single guy."

Sam didn't know what to say. Congratulations? How horrible? Neither seemed appropriate.

"Which made my stepfather's accusations even more ridiculous," Marcee said in a matter-of-fact tone.

Sam remembered his deputy's damning comments. He couldn't help but be curious about what really happened that night. "Ron mentioned that incident to me."

"Of course he did." Sam could hear the bitterness in her voice.

"Hey." His fingers curved under her chin and tipped it up. "I'm not judging you. I'm not sure what happened that night—"

"Camden was fussing." Normally Marcee wouldn't have considered explaining, but the acceptance she saw in Sam's eyes brought the words to her lips. "He wasn't hurt or anything."

"Ron said when your folks—"

"Not my folks," Marcee corrected. "Shirleen and my stepfather."

"He said when Shirleen and your stepfather got home they found you and your boyfriend without any clothes—"

To his surprise, Marcee laughed. "Ryan might have been pushing for a home run but he'd barely made it to second base."

"But your stepfather must have seen that it was all innocent."

"He turned around what he saw to suit his purpose," Marcee said with a shrug. "Shirleen deferred to his 'judgment' over the proper punishment."

"It had to be horrible, being kicked out of the only home you'd known." Sympathy filled Sam's eyes. "You were just a kid. Like Fern."

Marcee reached over and laid a comforting hand on his arm . . . as if he was the one who needed reassurance, not her. "It's okay."

"It's *not* okay," he said.

"It was a long time ago," Marcee said softly. "How 'bout we enjoy this beautiful day and do some hiking?"

She looked so pretty with the sunlight dancing across her hair that he felt he had to kiss her.

"Mmm," she said when his lips left hers. "Ever thought about doing it in the woods?"

"Hold that thought." Sam grabbed her hand. "There's a place I want to show you first. Apparently, kids go there for parties. It's a creek running though a canyon with sand beaches."

Marcee's gaze narrowed. "You're making that up."

"It's the truth, the whole truth, and nothing but the truth," Sam said, tugging her down the trail. "And it's definitely something you have to see to believe."

The tortuous trip down the steep incline made Marcee doubly glad she'd left the sandals at home. Sam went first but stopped every few feet to make sure she was okay.

Having been on her own for so long, she wasn't quite sure what to make of such solicitude. But the concern in his eyes was genuine and the protective way he reached out to lend a helping hand made her feel like something special. When she finally reached the bottom, her breath caught in her throat.

The place was every bit as beautiful as he'd promised. He'd called it a "canyon," but they were actually standing in the bottom of a creek bed. Thankfully, the side she and Sam had descended offered saplings they could hold onto and rocks they could use for footholds. The other side—a sheer dirt wall rising twenty feet straight up—wouldn't have been so hospitable.

Marcee inhaled deeply and took it all in. Sunlight danced across the ripples of the slow moving water in front of her. Other than a black bird cawing from a tree at the top of the opposite bank, silence surrounded them. She lifted her face to the sun. Sam had been right. If she hadn't seen it herself she would never have believed such a place existed. "This is unbelievable."

He took a step closer and looped an arm around her shoulder. "It's like being in our own little world."

Their eyes met and for a long moment time stood still. Then Marcee forced a laugh and kicked one of several beer cans lying in the gravel and sand at her feet. "Something tells me if we were here on a weekend night, our own little world might be pretty crowded."

Sam chuckled, his gaze lingering on the cans. "I think you're right."

Marcee shook her head. "I can't figure out how I could have lived in Ellwood for eighteen years and not known this place existed."

"Sometimes those things that are most special can be right under our nose." He stared at her, not sparing a glance at the scenery he was describing.

Marcee's heart rose to her throat. "Thank you for bringing me here."

"When Ron first showed it to me, I thought of you," he said in a deep husky voice.

She'd had men tell her a song or a particular perfume made them think of her, but never a piece of property. But the fact that he'd thought about her during the workday made it all the more special.

"Once I saw it, all I could think about was bringing you here and sharing it with you," he added.

Marcee smiled as his arms slipped around her neck. The heat of his body enveloped her and a now familiar anticipation made her heart skip a beat. But Sam didn't seem in any hurry. Instead, his gaze lingered on her face as if memorizing her features.

Then one hand moved up and his fingers gently slipped though her hair. "I want you to know there isn't anyone I'd rather have here with me."

His lips closed over hers and the familiar feeling of rightness rose inside her. And, for the first time, she let herself hope—just a little—in the fairy tale.

Fern glanced sideways at Cam. Since she hadn't wanted to take her dad's truck, she appointed Cam as the designated driver for the trip to Barrington. His sister's late model Jetta had been pulled into duty and was now headed down the freeway toward Chicago.

"Are you sure I'm not going to be in the way?" Cam asked.

Fern heaved an exasperated sigh. They'd already had this discussion when she invited him to go with her. "I told you. Annie won't care. She's going to love you."

Still, Cam didn't look convinced. "Remember

when we looked at those pictures? The ones from Annie's graduation party you posted on your MySpace page?"

Fern smiled and nodded. She loved posting photos of her friends online.

"When I was looking at the party pics, I didn't see anyone in those photos who looked like me," Cam said.

While it was true that the crowd she'd run with at Barrington High had been composed of mostly athletes and cheerleaders, Annie had been Fern's only good friend. What she and Annie shared went beyond liking to shop. Annie had been her supporter, her confidante, and, when her mother died, her rock.

That's why Fern hadn't balked when her father brought up moving to Ellwood. With Annie leaving for college in the fall, there wasn't anything in Barrington she'd miss.

"Not one person," Cam said.

Fern pulled her attention to the boy who'd become more important to her in the few weeks since they'd met than any of the guys she'd left behind. She couldn't believe how he had fixated on those pictures. If she could go back in time, she would never have shown them to him. "Are you still worried Annie won't like you?"

"I don't give a crap what she thinks," Cam said, a little too forcefully. "But seeing those pictures made me wonder about you. You're one of the beautiful people, Fern. You could be with anyone."

The compliment pleased her. She liked hearing that Cam found her attractive. Liked it a lot. But she didn't have a chance to focus on the pretty words because, while there was admiration in Cam's tone, there was something else there, too. It was that indescribable something that caused her to shift uneasily in her seat. "Thank you. I think."

Cam's fingers tightened around the steering wheel until his knuckles turned white. "Your friend is going to take one look at me and think you've gone off the deep end."

"How many times do I have to tell you Annie is going to love you?" This time as she said the words, Fern wondered if she was being totally honest. Annie would be nice, of course. But what would her stylish friend actually think about Cam's spiky hair and piercing?

There had been a group of boys who looked and dressed like Cam at Barrington High, and they weren't on her radar. In fact, Fern doubted she would have noticed Camden if he hadn't been her next door neighbor. And . . . if she hadn't been quite so lonely.

Though she'd railed against Sarah Beth's close-minded attitude, Fern knew she'd been guilty of the same kind of prejudice in the past. She'd seen a person with piercings and thought *drugs*. Not that the use of illegal drugs was confined to that social strata. She could name athletes and cheerleaders who used, but in her crowd the drug of choice had been alcohol.

Still, if she'd stayed in Barrington, Fern knew she would never have given a guy like Cam a second glance. She only hoped Anne wouldn't be so shallow.

She looped her arm through his. "Remember the day we met?"

"How could I forget?" A smile finally touched Cam's lips. "I was playing my bass on the deck, minding my own business, when you slipped through the back gate and interrupted my practice. You looked so pathetic I had to offer you a soda."

Fern giggled. She remembered that day very differently. She'd been taking out the trash when a melody of rich sounds wafted over the fence. After she dumped the garbage, she'd decided to be nosy and see who was playing such beautiful music.

She wasn't sure what she'd expected, but it sure

wasn't a tall, skinny boy about her age with a shock of red hair. He seemed eager to talk, and she accepted his offer of a soda because she had nothing better to do.

He'd put his bass aside and they sat in the deck chairs and talked. Fern had been amazed at how much they had in common. They enjoyed the same kind of music and were both voracious readers. It had been a hot day, and she quickly downed her Coke. When he went inside to get more, he brought out not only another soda, but a bag of chips for them to share. As they'd continued to talk, Fern discovered that Camden Smith was an intelligent and sensitive guy.

The feeling of camaraderie she'd experienced took her by surprise. She'd dated a lot. The guys had all been good-looking and popular, student leaders and athletes. But she felt closer to Cam that first day than to any of those guys. And she and Cam weren't even dating.

Fern leaned her head against his shoulder. When she told her dad she considered Cam to be a good friend, it had been true . . . at the time. But recently she'd begun to realize that the feelings she had for Cam went beyond simple friendship. "I'm so happy you came with me. I can't think of another person I'd rather spend the day with than you."

"Are you drunk?" Cam slanted a disbelieving glance her way while exiting the freeway.

Fern chuckled as he slowed the car to a stop at the light at the end of the off ramp. The strongest drink she'd had all morning had been iced tea. "Perhaps," she said. "I'm drunk on you."

She moistened her lips with the tip of her tongue and was rewarded when the green of his eyes changed from emerald to jade in a single heartbeat. As his arm slid around her and his lips lowered to hers, two words ran over and over in her head: *About time.*

Fern's lips were still tingling an hour later when she, Annie, and Cam entered a large discount store in Schaumberg. Annie wanted to come to the popular store to shop for dorm room junk. Fern hadn't cared where they went as long as it was out of Annie's house.

The introductions had gone well. Oh, there had been a momentary flicker of surprise in Annie's eyes when she'd first seen Cam, but she immediately rallied and her smile was warm and welcoming. Annie's parents, on the other hand, hadn't been quite so open-minded. Lloyd Carman stared with obvious disapproval at the ring in Cam's brow. Carol, Annie's mother, hadn't stared but with a bright smile asked if the "thing" on his face hurt.

Surprisingly, Cam took it all in stride. But when Annie mentioned that she was in the mood to shop, he'd been quick to agree.

"I want to look at some CD stacks." Cam glanced down at his watch. "How 'bout I meet you both back here in a half hour?"

Fern understood what he was doing and her heart rose to her throat. Cam knew it had been several weeks since she'd seen Annie, and this was his way of giving them time alone. She'd noticed he also carefully avoided touching her in any way. It was as if he was giving her the option of telling Annie that they were just friends.

And up until the kiss—er, kisses—they'd shared in the car, that's all they had been. But she didn't kiss boys who were just her friends. The feelings Cam had stirred in the car elevated their relationship to a different level.

"Fern." Annie's voice pulled her back to the present, and she realized that Cam and Annie were both awaiting her response. "Is that okay with you?"

Her gaze shifted from her supremely confident friend to Cam, who stood off to the side, his hands shoved into the pockets of his oversized olive green cargo pants.

All she had to do was say the word and he would disappear for a half hour. But she already knew him well enough to know that he would spend the next thirty minutes wondering if his meeting her friend had changed things between them. Though many girls liked to keep their guys guessing, she had never been into such games.

"Sounds good," she said to Annie. "There's just one thing I need to do first."

Turning to Cam, Fern took a step closer and wrapped her arms around his neck. Without saying another word she pressed her lips against his and kissed him. Not a kiss you would give a good friend, but the kind of kiss a girl gives to a guy she's crazy about.

After a moment's hesitation, Cam's arms slid around her waist. He pulled her close, kissing her back. By the time he released her, Fern's head was spinning and her breathing was ragged. His hand lingered for a moment on her arm and she noticed the smile had returned to his face. "See ya in thirty."

When he walked away, it was with the firm, confident stride of a man who knows his place in the world . . . and in his girlfriend's heart. Fern's lips curved up in satisfaction. She watched until he was out of sight before turning back to Annie. "What did you want to look at first?"

"Bedspreads," Annie murmured, a dazed look on her face, then shook her head as if trying to make sense of what she'd just witnessed.

"What color were you thinking?" Fern asked. "Something bright and fun? Or a little more subtle?"

"I don't know." Annie waved a dismissive hand. "I don't care about comforters. What was *that*?"

Fern feigned innocence. "I'm not sure what you mean."

"You kissed him."

"I did," Fern said, no longer able to keep from smiling.

"I thought you were just friends."

"Why would you think that?"

"Because that's what you told me." Annie's voice rose with each word, and an older couple walking by turned to stare. Annie stared right back and the two looked away. Only then did her friend refocus.

"You have to admit," Annie said in a lower, more reasonable tone, "he's nothing like the other guys you've dated."

"You're right," Fern agreed happily. "He isn't."

A skeptical look crossed Annie's face.

"Cam might not be drop dead gorgeous," Fern said, "but I think he's sexy. He's also smart and funny and good to me. He has all the qualities I want in a boyfriend."

Annie opened her mouth then shut it without speaking.

"It's important to me that you like him," Fern said.

"I do like him," Annie said with a decisive nod. An impish look suddenly filled her blue eyes. "I can't say as much for my dad. Did you see the look on his face when Cam walked through the door?"

Fern giggled. "I'm sure he was thinking better me than you."

"Probably." Annie laughed. "Speaking of dads, what does yours think of Cam?"

Fern picked up a heavy bookend from a nearby table and shifted it in her hand, her smile fading. "At first he didn't want me having anything to do with Cam. Now he's backed off. But I think deep down he's hoping I find a guy more like the ones I used to date. What he doesn't understand is that Cam is a much better person than any of them."

Fern carefully settled the bookend back on the

table, wondering how her father could be so smart about some things and so stupid about others.

"Maybe he'll like Cam more once he sees how happy he makes you," Annie said encouragingly as they ambled down the wide aisle.

"Maybe," Fern said, her heart heavy. For a few seconds it had been so easy to forget how her father felt about Cam.

Annie stopped in front of a display of picture frames. "Does your dad like small town life?"

Fern shook her head. "I don't think so. Though he is home a lot more."

A frame decorated with an assortment of brightly colored stones drew Fern's attention. She picked it up and flipped it over to see the price. Surprised that it was well under the amount she had in her wallet, she held it up to Annie. "What do you think of this one?"

Annie studied the frame. "Cool. What would you put in it?"

"The picture of me you took at the White Sox game," Fern said. "To give to Cam."

"Smart girl." Annie tapped a finger against her temple. "He puts the frame at the bedside and your beautiful face is the last thing he sees before he goes to bed and the first when he wakes up."

A warmth welled up inside Fern. What had she ever done to deserve such a supportive friend? "I've missed you, Annie."

"Ditto." Annie flashed a smile. "I can't wait until this next year is over. Then you'll join me at Northwestern and it'll be like it used to be."

Fern wished she could believe that things could be as they once were . . . but she had the feeling that even if she did join Annie in a year, they would both be different people. Of course, she reminded herself, different didn't always translate into bad. Look at Cam . . .

"Speaking of Northwestern," Fern said, tucking the frame under her arm, "we have some shopping to do."

Thirty minutes passed quickly, and they reconnected with Cam. Fern wrapped her bag around the frame so Cam wouldn't see it and kept it that way as the three of them walked around the store and shopped. By the time they'd made it through the whole store, Annie and Cam were laughing and talking like old friends.

"What do you think about going to the Cheesecake Factory for dinner?" Annie asked. "There's one just across the parking lot from here."

Fern turned to Cam, and he nodded.

"Sounds good to us," Fern said, liking the feel of the last word on her tongue.

"Great." Annie glanced down at her cart. The only thing she'd found was a bookcase. Though it looked pretty big, Cam had assured Annie that the box would fit in the Saturn's trunk. "Do you think they'll have a clerk available to carry this out for me?"

"No worries," Cam said. "I'll help you with it."

"Thank you, kind sir," Annie said, flashing him a bright smile.

Fern felt an unexpected twist of jealousy. But the smile Cam shot the pretty blonde was friendly, nothing more.

"What about you?" he asked Fern. "Are you buying anything?"

"I'm not sure." Fern clutched her bag and the still hidden picture frame against her chest. "I thought I'd look around while you two check out and get that in the car."

"We can wait," Cam said. "What do you want to look at?"

Fern lifted her shoulder in a slight shrug and cast a pointed glance at Annie then down at her bag. "I just want to check out a few things."

"C'mon, Cam," Annie said. "I think I hear thunder. I don't want to be dragging this out to the car in the rain."

Still, Cam hesitated, his gaze searching Fern's eyes. "We'll be right out front."

"I'll be five minutes behind you, tops," Fern assured him.

He leaned over and brushed her lips with his. "See you soon."

Fern lingered behind as the two headed to the checkout area. She wandered over to the kitchen area, drawn to a large green and white mixer. This heavy duty monster had been her mother's dream machine. She shifted her purse to her other arm, caressing the smooth surface with her fingers.

Tears stung her eyes. Her mother had never gotten the mixer. Money had been tight, and she had been selected for a middle school cheering squad. The money her mother had set aside for the appliance went for the uniform instead. When Fern had halfheartedly protested that she didn't need to be on the squad, her mother said she'd get her mixer for Christmas. But by Thanksgiving she'd been gone.

Fern closed her eyes as a familiar ache filled her chest. Would this pain ever go away? Would she ever stop aching for what was lost? Her only consolation was that she could now go months, instead of days, without being blindsided by grief. *I'm so sorry, Mommy. I wish you could have had everything you wanted.*

"Honey." A gentle hand touched her shoulder. "Are you okay?"

Fern opened her eyes to find an older gray-haired woman staring at her with a worried expression. Feeling a wetness on her cheeks, Fern quickly brushed the tears away with her fingers. She drew a ragged breath. "I'm fine."

The woman hesitated, apparently unconvinced.

Fern forced a smile. "Really. I'm fine."

The ringing of the cell phone in her shirt pocket saved her from having to say more. She wiggled her fingers good-bye to the woman, pulled the phone from her pocket and flipped it open. "Hello."

"Where are you?" Annie asked. "The wind has picked up and the sky is really black. It looks like it's going to start raining any minute. If you don't get out here soon, you're going to get soaked."

"I'm on my way." Casting one last look at the mixer, Fern hurried to the front of the store, thoughts of her mother still swirling in her head.

She could hear the thunder as the automatic doors leading outside opened, and she quickened her step. She'd just stepped onto the curb when someone grabbed her arm from behind.

"Hey," she said, trying her best to pull away but failing. "Let go of me."

She turned, fully prepared to start screaming if the pervert didn't let her go. Then she saw the uniform, the badge, and the grim expression on the officer's face.

Fern suddenly realized she'd walked out without paying for the picture frame. A knot formed in the pit of her stomach. Her perfect day had taken a decidedly bad turn.

18

"I wonder how Cam and Fern are doing in Chicago," Marcee said in a relaxed, conversational tone. "It's supposed to hit a hundred today."

Sam uncorked the bottle of wine. While he still had his reservations over Fern spending so much time with Cam, he had to admit the boy was growing on him. He liked Cam's respectful attitude toward Fern and the fact that Fern was always home on time when she was with Cam.

Not to mention that allowing their friendship to flourish had given him more time with Marcee. Two weeks had passed since he first took Marcee to "the woods," and while finding time during the week had been difficult, they were able to spend at least one weekend day together.

There had been several events in town they could have gone to, but Sam was selfish. He knew if they went to an Ellwood function, he'd have to share her with her rapidly growing network of friends. And the time he spent with Marcee was too precious. Instead, he and Marcee had concentrated on exploring the Old Plank Trail south of Chicago. That's where they'd been most of today. On their way back into town Marcee suggested getting a beer at a popular local tavern, but he'd nixed the idea. He had something more romantic in mind.

After briefly stopping at her house so she could grab a change of clothes, they'd returned to his house and taken a long, leisurely shower . . . together. Marcee's hair now hung to her shoulders in slightly damp waves.

The simple sleeveless dress she'd pulled on wasn't overtly sexy, but Sam knew just what was beneath that light cotton fabric and his body reacted as if she were naked. But there would be time for that later.

"I thought it'd be romantic to have a picnic supper on the floor." The minute the words left his mouth Sam worried that his lack of experience with women was showing. "A little wine. Some cheese. A whole lotta me?"

Thankfully, Marcee didn't laugh. Instead she settled gracefully on the blanket he'd spread on the floor. "Why, Sheriff, it sounds like I may have myself a poet."

Sam thought about protesting but the look in her eyes told him that being a poet was a very, very good thing. So instead he smiled. "I have the wine chilling," he said. "How about some music?"

Marcee glanced at the clock sitting on the fireplace. "What time do you expect Fern?"

"Not until nine," he said. "If I know my daughter, she won't walk through that door one second sooner."

"There's so much to do in Chicago." Marcee's tone turned wistful.

Rather than pour the wine, Sam sat on the floor next to her. "Sounds like you miss it."

"I do. Not as much as when I first moved here, but I love city life." While she was becoming acclimated to Ellwood, she wasn't sure she'd ever love it like her friends Paula and Iris did. "Don't you miss Chicago?"

For a second Sam was tempted to give his pat answer. The one he kept handy when anyone asked him how he liked Ellwood. The politically correct answer. The lie. Until he remembered that this was Marcee, one of the few people he could trust with his true feelings.

"I do," he said. "I miss the excitement, the faster pace. Hell, I even miss my neighbors. While they were friendly, they didn't seem to feel the need to know every facet of my personal life. Not like they do here."

"I miss all the things there are to do in a big city." Marcee's eyes took on a faraway look. "Places to shop, to eat. Did you know I used to check out a different ethnic restaurant every week and try the strangest sounding dish on the menu?"

"An adventuress," Sam said with a smile. "Why doesn't that surprise me?"

Sam thought of all the fun they'd had in the shower and realized that in every part of her life, Marcee seized the moment and made the time special.

"What kind of ethnic cuisine do you like?" Marcee asked.

Sam shrugged. "I haven't tried enough to really know. I think about checking out something new but in the end I end up ordering the same old stand-bys."

"Pastrami on rye?"

Sam grinned. "You know me too well."

"Sometimes you just have to do it," Marcee said, sounding surprisingly serious. "Step outside that comfort zone."

Sam lifted a brow.

"You've only been in town a month, yet you already have a place you go every Sunday for breakfast," she pointed out. "My guess is you even order the same thing every week."

"I happen to like the food at the Grateful Bread," Sam said, trying not to sound defensive. "You know as well as I do that there aren't that many places in town—"

"There's more than one," Marcee said, not giving an inch.

"C'mon, you have to admit you like a certain routine in your life, too," he said, sweetening the words with a smile. "We all do."

"You're right," she acknowledged. "And there are certain routines I wouldn't want to give up."

Sam hoped she was referring to their nightly phone conversations. Talking to her right before he drifted off to sleep had become a most pleasurable habit. He'd tell her about his day and learn about hers. Sometimes he'd discuss issues at work, trusting that what he said wouldn't go any further. Though she discounted her impact, she had remarkable insight into human emotions, and just talking to her lifted his spirits.

While he didn't believe in all that soul-mate crap, he and Marcee were definitely on the same wavelength. In fact, he wasn't sure he'd be able to sleep now without hearing her voice.

"Routine is one thing," Marcee said, her words breaking into his thoughts. "Being in a rut is different."

"You think I'm in a rut?" The disappointment that gripped his chest told him how important her opinion had become to him.

"We all get into ruts." Marcee leaned forward and trailed a finger up his arm, "But in a way, that's part of your appeal."

The desire that had been satiated less than an hour earlier returned. But Sam did his best to ignore it and concentrated on her words. "Being in a rut is part of my appeal?"

She smiled. "What I meant was that you're steady and true, someone a woman can count on."

Sam twisted his lips in a wry smile. "Just call me Fido."

"I'm serious." She gave his arm a punch. "Before you give your heart to someone, you have to trust them."

Sam stilled. His feelings for Marcee had deepened so quickly that he hadn't been sure if she felt the same. Was this her way of telling him she was falling for him, too?

He grabbed her hand and brought it to his lips. "Have I told you lately how glad I am that you're here with me?"

Her lips twitched. "You've shown me . . . quite a few times."

He chuckled and pulled her to him just as a familiar melody filled the air.

"Fern," he told Marcee. "Hopefully wanting to extend her curfew."

He pulled the phone from his pocket. "Hi, honey. Having a good time?"

"Daddy," she said. "Someone wants to talk to you."

Her voice trembled, and though he couldn't be sure, it sounded as though she'd been crying. Sam tightened his grip on the phone and forced himself to breathe.

"Sam," a deep voice sounded on the other end of the phone. "This is Larry Krasnowski."

Sam's blood turned to ice. When he was a

young officer patrolling the streets of South Chicago, Larry had been his partner. Though they'd lost touch, as far as Sam knew, Larry was still on the force.

"Is my daughter okay?" Sam demanded, myriad images flashing in his head, each one more awful than the last. "Has there been an accident?"

"No accident," Larry said. "I don't know if you heard but I'm doing some off-duty security work at a retail store in Schaumberg on weekends."

Sam bit back an expletive. Fern had called crying and his old partner wanted to make small talk. "What does that have to do with my daughter?"

"Caught her shoplifting," Larry said bluntly, finally getting down to business. "I was going to call the police but when she told me her name, I made the connection. I'm letting her go this time. But I thought you should know."

"I can't believe it." Sam's thoughts tumbled wildly in his head. Fern stealing? Unbelievable. "She's never even had a parking ticket. Fern's a good kid, Larry."

"She tried to tell me she'd gotten distracted and forgot to pay—"

"I *did* forget," Sam heard his daughter say in the background.

"She seems sincere," Larry said grudgingly. He

lowered his voice. "But I gotta tell you, when I saw the boy who was waiting for her in the car, red flags started popping up. You do what you want—I mean she's your kid and all—but if I were you, I'd take a good look at the type of company your girl is keeping."

Sam's fingers clenched the phone. Disappointment warred with relief followed by a healthy dose of anger. "Thank you, buddy. I owe you big-time."

"No problem," Larry said. "Do you want to talk to her again?"

"No," Sam said. "I'll save what I have to say for when she gets home."

"What happened?" Marcee asked as soon as he hung up. "Are Fern and Cam okay?"

Sam jerked to his feet, unable to process what he'd heard. Exhaling a harsh breath, he moved to the fireplace and placed both hands on the mantel. "It's not good."

Marcee scrambled to her feet and moved to his side. She hadn't been too worried because, though she'd sensed there had been some trouble, Sam remained calm. But now the muscle in his jaw was hopping like a Mexican jumping bean and his knuckles were white.

"Tell me," she demanded. "Everything."

Sam whirled, hot anger rising inside him. He and Fern had talked at length about this very issue not two years ago. One of her friends had fallen in with a bad crowd and was caught stealing. Fern had sworn she'd never done such a thing, would never do such a thing. And he'd believed her. "Fern was caught shoplifting."

The pain in his voice seared Marcee's heart. For a second she could only stare. Finally able to rally her thoughts, she took a step closer. "I don't believe it. Whoever told you that is lying."

"She was caught red-handed." Sam had spent his life formulating conclusions based on evidence. Though he desperately wanted to believe Fern, he couldn't change the facts.

"Still—"

"It was a former partner of mine who caught her." He released his death grip on the mantel and turned. Embarrassment mingled with anger. "He recognized the name. When he found out she was my daughter, he let her go."

"There has to be more to the story." While Marcee wasn't sure what had happened, she was certain that Fern was no thief. "What did she say?"

"That it was a mistake." Sam raked a hand through his hair and began to pace the room. "She said she got distracted and forgot to pay."

Marcee thought of all the times she'd been talking and almost walked out with unpaid merchandise. She nodded. "Makes sense."

The same thought had crossed Sam's mind, but it seemed too pat, too convenient. "Don't tell me you believe that bullshit?"

His comment, and his tone, was so similar to the words her stepfather had uttered to Shirleen that Marcee's blood ran cold.

She told herself this was a shock to him. Sam was a nice guy, a good dad. He just needed to calm down and think more clearly. "Of course I do," she said in as neutral a tone as she could muster. "Don't you?"

The tight mask that covered Sam's face gave nothing away, but bleakness filled his hazel eyes. "I'm not sure what I believe. My gut says to believe her, but I don't want to be a fool, either."

Marcee felt the tension in her shoulders ease. For a second she'd worried he might be as unreasonable as her stepfather.

"She's a good girl, Sam." She moved to him and placed a reassuring hand on his arm. "Good values. Good friends—"

"She *had* good friends." Sam's lips twisted. "Until I moved her here."

He couldn't stop feeling like he was to blame.

Fern had been at loose ends since they moved to Ellwood. No cheerleading practice. No parties at the lake with the girls. Only time with Camden.

"She'll make friends here," Marcee said confidently. "And she and Annie are still close."

"Larry was right," Sam continued as if she hadn't spoken. "I should have paid more attention to who she was hanging out with. I'm the parent. It's my responsibility to make sure she didn't get involved with kids who are a bad influence."

Marcee wasn't sure who Larry was or why his opinion mattered, but obviously he had Sam all stirred up. "But she isn't, I mean, she hasn't gotten in with the wrong crowd. The only one she's been spending time with is Cam."

"Bingo." Sam couldn't believe that the boy had snowed him. He'd actually thought the kid had a good head on his shoulders.

Normally quick on the uptake, it took Marcee a few seconds to get what Sam was saying. The realization came like a slap to her face.

He's had a shock. He's not thinking clearly.

She pressed her lips together to still the sharp words poised on the tip of her tongue and dug her nails into her palms.

"It sounds like you're blaming Cam," she said finally in her most reasonable tone. "But that's an easy out and you know it. You don't even know what happened."

Marcee found herself hoping that Sam would protest, tell her she'd misunderstood, that he hadn't played judge and jury on circumstantial evidence—hell, on *no* evidence—and found her brother guilty.

"Open your eyes." Sam found himself speaking more loudly than was necessary, considering she was right beside him. But his control was slipping and his rioting emotions were becoming more difficult to contain. "Look at his hair. Look at that piercing—"

"Look at what a good decent kid he is." Marcee raised her voice to match his level. "He wouldn't steal and he wouldn't encourage Fern to do that, either."

"I bet the majority of people in this town would say otherwise."

"Well, the majority of people in this town would say I'm a horrible person and a slut," Marcee shot back.

Sam stilled, too shocked to respond. Then he clenched his hands into fists. *No one better say such lies within his hearing.* "If anyone thinks that, they're wrong."

"And they're wrong about Cam." *You're wrong*

about Cam. "Your daughter is a great kid. So is my brother."

For a second Sam's tightly held control seemed to crumble, and Marcee caught a glimpse of his despair. It gave her hope. He loved Fern, and she believed, given the chance, he'd do the right thing.

"Listen to your daughter," she said finally. "Give her a chance to explain before you jump to any conclusions. Then believe what she says. Trust that she's being honest with you. After all, she's never given you any reason to doubt her."

"You don't have kids," Sam said, wanting so much to believe in Fern but not wanting to play the fool. "You don't know . . . "

"Don't know what?" Marcee's last remaining thread of patience began to fray. "That you're hurt and embarrassed that your daughter got picked up by the cops?"

She wanted nothing more than to walk out the door and let him handle the situation as he saw fit. But that's what her mother had done . . . with disastrous results.

While she knew that Sam wouldn't physically harm Fern, a few careless words could easily ruin the relationship they'd started to build. The way he responded to his daughter tonight was critical.

The experience could either draw them closer or push them apart.

Knowing what it was like to be estranged from her only parent, she didn't want that for Fern. And Sam, well, there was no doubt in her mind that losing Fern's love and respect would devastate him. So instead of heading for the door, she kept her feet firmly planted.

"Even though I hated my stepfather, it still hurt that he didn't believe me," Marcee said. "Don't make the same mistake with Fern."

For several seconds a flicker deep in the back of Sam's eyes was his only response. "I don't want her hanging out with Cam anymore."

It didn't take a genius to realize what was happening. Sam was transferring *his* guilt over being an absentee dad to her brother. "You haven't even heard—"

"I have to do what I think is best for my daughter." Sam cursed the tremor in his voice, the uncertainty in his tone.

"You've never thought Cam was good enough for Fern," Marcee said. "You're using this incident as an excuse."

"It's *my* decision, Marcee."

"You don't think Cam is good enough for Fern," Marcee repeated. The confusion in his eyes didn't fool her one bit. "You have a certain type of guy in mind for Fern. One like Ted Dees. Even though you don't know Ted. Even though you don't know the kind of boy he is . . . "

"The way people act and dress gives us a clue," Sam shot back, wondering why Marcee was bringing up a kid he didn't even know. Surely she realized if he had his way, Fern wouldn't be dating at all. "Sloppy clothes, spiky hair, and piercings at the very least say the kid is making a nonconformist statement. Tell me that isn't true."

"Cam isn't like that—"

"Then why does he dress and act that way?"

"Because he wants to be noticed," Marcee responded, then stopped for a second wondering if she'd just been describing Cam or herself. "Until someone notices, there's no chance they'll care."

Marcee suddenly realized it had been the reason she'd flaunted her sexuality. Her behavior had been an adolescent's way of coping. But somehow the pattern had continued into adulthood . . .

"There may be a nice kid beneath Cam's 'to hell with you' appearance," Sam said, gentling his words when he saw the stress on her face. "But I don't know that, and after today I can't take that chance."

His gaze slid to the blanket on the floor, lingered on the wine chilling in the silver bucket. "I'd better get this stuff put away."

"Yeah," Marcee taunted. "Wouldn't want Fern to find out what you spent the afternoon doing."

"Marcee." Sam rubbed a hand across his face, all of a sudden weary. "Not now . . . please."

She wanted to be angry with him. But she couldn't. She knew him. Knew how much pressure he put on himself to be a good dad. Knew how guilty he felt now . . . and how alone. Impulsively, she wrapped her arms around him and drew him close.

For a second he stiffened, and she thought he might push her away. But after a moment she felt the tension leave his body and his arms slide around her waist.

"You'll do the right thing," she whispered against his chest. "You're a good father."

"Sometimes I don't think so," Sam said, wondering why kids didn't come with a rule book . . . why everything had to be so hard.

"It's not the good times that define us," Marcee said softly. "It's how we respond to the bad."

She wasn't sure where she'd heard the saying, only that it seemed to fit the situation.

Sam leaned his head against hers and exhaled a breath. "Thank you."

Marcee reveled in the closeness, finding the warm embrace as intimate as making love. "I didn't do anything."

"You're a good friend," he said softly. "You cared enough to make me step back and think."

In the past when a man had told her she was "a friend," it signaled the beginning of the end. But she had the feeling that this time it might mean the beginning of a new . . . deeper . . . more meaningful relationship with Sam McKelvey.

19

"*Thanks for parking here,*" *Fern said to Cam.*

Instead of having Cam pull into her driveway, she'd asked him to park at the end of the block. Cam had, and without asking a single question.

He shrugged. "I'm in no hurry to get home."

They stood on the sidewalk at the end of the block. Fern could see her house. The truck was parked in the driveway so she knew her dad was home. "I just need a few minutes to get myself together."

She'd embarrassed herself by crying most of the drive home. Thankfully, Cam had been cool about the meltdown. He'd held her hand and said all the right things.

"I'll go in with you," he said. "I can explain how I had Annie call to tell you the weather was getting worse and that we'd rushed you—"

"It wasn't your fault." She had never been one to blame others for her own actions, and she wasn't about to start now. "I just forgot about the picture frame."

"He'll understand that." Cam looped a comforting arm around her shoulder and gave a little squeeze. "We all make mistakes."

"Not my dad." Fern put her hands together to still the trembling. "He's going to be pissed."

Actually, the anger wasn't what worried her, it was facing his disappointment.

Cam grew still. "He'd better not hurt you."

For a second Fern wasn't sure what Cam meant. Then she remembered him telling her how he'd been happy when his father had left, happy because he was tired of getting hit anytime he did anything wrong.

"He won't touch me." Fern laid a reassuring hand on Cam's arm then gave a halfhearted laugh. "Though he might yell."

Cam's eyes flashed emerald fire. "He better not."

"It'll be okay," Fern said with more confidence than she felt. While she and her father had made great strides in getting to know each other, in some ways he was still a stranger.

She knew he wouldn't hit her, but other than that, she wasn't sure how he would react. Would he listen to her side? Or just start yelling and ground her?

They walked slowly in silence for several moments.

"I liked Annie," Cam said, as if trying to get her mind off what awaited her at the end of the block. "She's cool."

"Cooler than me?" Fern kept her tone light.

Boys always liked Annie. Sometimes it was hard having a friend who was so pretty and fun.

Cam snorted and the look in his eyes made her smile. "There's no one cooler than you."

Fern's heart filled with an emotion she couldn't begin to identify. Her throat grew tight and she found herself once again blinking back tears. "Thank you, Cam."

His eyes widened in surprise. "For what?"

"For being so good to me." It was an understatement, but she didn't know what else to say. Thanks for believing in me? For letting me cry on your shoulder? For listening to my worries?

"I'd do anything for you, Fern," Cam said

in a low, soft tone. "If you ever need me, I'll be there."

The warmth that rose inside Fern was tinged with regret. "I'm sorry I screwed up the day. We could be at the Cheesecake Factory right now, laughing and having fun—"

"Yeah, but then it'd be the three of us." Cam shot her a wink and tucked her hand through his arm. "This way I have you all to myself."

Impulsively, Fern leaned over and brushed a kiss against his cheek.

Cam grinned. "That's exactly what I'm liking."

She laughed and felt her spirits rise. The happiness lasted until she reached her driveway.

"Let me come in with you," Cam said, his eyes dark with concern.

Fern slid her hand from his arm. "Thanks, but I need to do this myself."

He stared at her for a long moment, then leaned forward and kissed her oh so gently. "Call me. Soon as you can."

"Absolutely." She shifted her gaze to the front door. A shiver of dread traveled up her spine.

"I'll be in your back pocket," Cam said.

Fern turned back and tilted her head questioningly.

Cam's face reddened. "It means I'm right there

with you. Even when you can't see me, I'm there."

Patting her back pocket, she squared her shoulders and headed toward the door.

Once Marcee left, Sam returned the blanket to the closet and the wine to the cupboard. Then he went upstairs and picked up the clothes he'd left strewn across the floor earlier on the way to the shower . . . with Marcee.

Marcee. What would he have done without her? When he first saw her at the wedding comforting the little boy, he'd known that she was something special. But until this evening he hadn't realized how special. Sure, she was fun and smart and sexy as hell, but there was a depth to her that she'd only recently begun to let him see. He was liking her more every day. Shit, who was he kidding? He was falling in love with her.

He laughed. Love was the last thing he'd been looking for when he went to that wedding. Or when he moved to Ellwood.

What had the minister said in church on Sunday? Things happened in God's time, not our own. Sam's lips lifted in a wry smile. Certainly seemed to be true in this situation.

But he didn't have time to think about what it meant now. He had important things to consider. Like Fern. And Camden Smith.

Maybe it *was* a coincidence that Fern—who'd never given him or Laura a moment of trouble— suddenly found herself on the other side of the law . . . but he didn't think so. As a parent it was his duty to protect her.

The boy was obviously a bad influence. He could only hope that given time and distance and the start of the school year, Fern would agree.

After glancing at his watch, Sam headed downstairs. His daughter should be home anytime now. He hadn't been sure where to have this heart-to-heart but finally decided on the kitchen. The large spacious room was one of Fern's favorite places to hang out when she was home.

He'd just dropped a couple of place mats and two glasses of milk on the table when he heard a key in the front door.

"Fern," he called out when the door creaked open. "Please come into the kitchen."

His voice came out more stern than he'd intended and her steps stilled. Damn. Fern hadn't even made it into the room and he was already screwing up.

Sam took several deep breaths, willing himself to relax. He'd barely exhaled the third breath when Fern appeared in the doorway.

"Hi, Daddy." The smile that normally hovered on the edges of her lips was conspicuously absent and her eyes were red-rimmed. Though he hated seeing his little girl so unhappy, it was reassuring to see she was taking the situation seriously.

Sam gestured to the table and put the sandwich he'd just cut on a plate. "I made each of us a ham and cheese sandwich. Thought you might be hungry."

She stared at him for a long moment, her gaze searching his, the wary look in her eyes making him sad.

"Thanks," she said finally, moving to the table. "We didn't have time to eat."

He put the plates on the table and took a seat opposite Fern. Though the cop in him wanted to slam his fist on the tabletop and demand some answers, he held back.

He brought the sandwich slowly to his lips, as if they had all the time in the world, and took a bite. The meat and cheese were fresh but tasted like sawdust. Still, he forced himself to chew and swallow. He picked up the glass of milk and took a long drink.

Fern nibbled on the edge of her sandwich and

stared up at him through lowered lashes. Finally, unable to wait any longer, Sam pushed the plate aside and leaned forward, resting his elbows on the table. "What were you thinking?"

The question sounded more like an accusation, and Fern flinched.

Swallowing his frustration at his inability to keep his cool, Sam reached across the table and took her hand. "Honey, tell me what happened. Help me to understand."

To his horror, tears filled her eyes and spilled down her cheeks. "It was a mistake . . . "

The sandwiches were forgotten as Fern continued to talk. Sam heard every little detail of the afternoon. When she got to the part about the green and white mixer, his heart twisted. He could see the appliance in his mind. Laura had shown it to him often enough. He, too, had known how much she wanted it, yet did nothing to make her dream a reality.

Granted, money had been tight, but he could have worked a couple more off-duty jobs and bought it for her . . .

"Then the police officer, I mean, the security guard, said I could go," Fern said.

Sam pulled his thoughts back to the matter at

hand. "You do realize that if it hadn't been for Larry you'd be facing shoplifting charges."

"I know." Fern lowered her eyes to the sandwich, then lifted them to meet his gaze. "But it was simply a mistake. I'm not a thief. You believe me, don't you?"

Sam thought of Marcee and her stepfather. It had hurt her when the man refused to believe her explanation. And it was something she'd never forgotten . . .

"I believe you," Sam said, hoping he wasn't being one of those heads-in-the-sand parents he used to curse, the ones who believed their kids never did anything wrong. But he reminded himself that this wasn't just any kid, this was *Fern.* "You've never given me any reason *not* to trust you. Just promise you'll pay more attention in the future."

A blindingly bright smile was his answer. She pushed back her chair and rose, rounding the table. Her arms wrapped around his neck in a tight hug.

"I told Cam you'd believe me. He was so worried." Fern's words tumbled out one after another. "I can't wait to call him."

"Honey . . . " Sam pushed back his chair and stood. "About Cam—"

Fern whirled in the doorway, the smile still on her lips. "What about him?"

"I think it's best if you don't see him anymore."

Her face paled. "Why? Next to Annie, Cam is my best friend."

Sam wished he could get away with just saying, *Because I said so*, but he knew Fern would never accept that reason. "What am I to think?" Sam asked gently. "You were never in any trouble until you met him."

When Fern crossed her arms and lifted her chin, any hope he'd harbored of her accepting his dictate quietly vanished. "He didn't have anything to do with today. I told you what happened. You said you believed me."

There was a challenge in her tone and more than a hint of disappointment.

"I do believe you—" he began.

"No, you don't," Fern interrupted. "Or you wouldn't be blaming Cam. Annie was there, too. Are you going to forbid me from seeing her?"

The rational part of Sam understood the point she was trying to make. But the dad part of him insisted he go to any lengths to keep her safe.

"Fern," he said, "I *do* believe you. But I'm your

father and I've lived a lot longer than you. You're going to have to trust me on this one."

He'd spoken in as reasonable a tone as he could muster, but anger flared in her eyes just the same.

"Cam is a good guy. One of the best I've ever known." Fern's voice, though low and controlled, shook with emotion. "I don't understand why you're being like this."

The look on her face tore at his heartstrings. He didn't want to be unreasonable. He just wanted to protect his little girl . . .

Damn. Was he being a savvy cop or just an over-protective dad? Was it Cam who'd twisted his gut into knots or would *any* boy have him thinking and feeling this way?

"It's been a long day," he said finally, his emotions too raw and his brain too muddled to rationally pursue this topic further. "How 'bout we discuss this later, when we're both rested and thinking more clearly?"

Fern brushed back strands of hair from her face with a sweeping gesture. Though she didn't say any more, the way she stood with her shoulders back and her head high reminded Sam of himself. The McKelveys were a stubborn lot, and he couldn't count the number of times he'd let Laura go to bed angry . . . determined not to give an inch, convinced his way was the right way. But he was older now and hopefully wiser.

Crossing the room, he stopped in front of Fern and offered a conciliatory smile. "I love you, Fern. I don't want you to ever doubt that."

The words had barely left his lips when she was in his arms.

"I love you, too, Daddy," she whispered against his chest. "But please don't say that I can't see Cam. Please."

Sam stroked the back of her head and kept his mouth shut. Because right now that was one promise he couldn't make.

Upstairs, Fern filled the large clawfoot tub
and settled into the scented water. While she
knew Cam was waiting to hear what had happened, she needed to figure out her father's
Jekyll and Hyde performance first. Her dad had
been a real sweetheart, understanding and kind
. . . until he turned on Cam, who'd done absolutely nothing wrong.

The only thing she could figure was that he had
felt the need to blame someone and chosen Cam. It
wasn't the most logical response, but whoever said
parents were rational? Still, if her dad thought she

was going to quit seeing Cam just because he said so, he had a lot to learn. She was almost eighteen and more than capable of choosing her own boy-friends, thank you very much.

Fern laid her head against the back of the tub and hit speed dial on her cell phone. As she'd ex-pected, Cam answered on the first ring.

"How did it go?" he asked eagerly, not bother-ing with hello.

"More good than bad." Fern went on to give him a blow-by-blow, stopping right before her father's ridiculous dictate.

She heard Cam exhale a relieved breath.

"I visualized him going off the deep end and being totally unreasonable," Cam said. "Sounds like he didn't go down that path after all."

"I wouldn't say that," Fern muttered under her breath.

"Fern?" Concern filled Cam's voice. "Is there something you're not telling me?"

Fern sank deeper into the water. Obviously she'd spoken louder than she intended. "My dad may have said one or two crazy things."

"Such as . . . ?"

"That I couldn't see you anymore." Fern con-tinued quickly before Cam got the wrong idea.

"But I told him no way was that happening and he backed down."

"Your father said you couldn't see me then all of a sudden he was okay with it?"

Even over the phone Fern could hear Cam's skepticism. It shouldn't have surprised her. His keen intelligence was one of the things that had first attracted her to him.

"He actually said we'd talk about it later. He'll come around." She interjected as much confidence into that statement as she could, not wanting Cam to worry.

"What if he doesn't change his mind?" Cam asked, his voice low and tight with control.

"No worries," Fern said. "Give him a few days. He'll chill and then everything will be back to normal."

"Sure?"

"Positive," Fern said firmly, pushing aside any of her own doubts.

"It's probably for the best that I'm headed to Chicago in the morning . . . " he murmured as if thinking aloud.

Fern jerked upright in the tub, sending water sloshing over the sides. "You're leaving? For how long?"

"Just until Thursday," Cam said. "It's a youth symphony event. Mandatory."

"You didn't say anything about it today." To Fern's dismay, her words sounded more accusatory than a mere statement of fact.

"I forgot all about it until I got home and the memo popped up on my computer," Cam said.

"I can't believe you're going to be gone all week." She couldn't keep the disappointment from her voice.

"Not *all* week," Cam clarified. "Just until Thursday night. I'll come right over when I get back. That's assuming your father will let me through the front door."

"He'll let—" Fern stopped, then groaned. "Oh no. My dad and I are having dinner at Paula Dees's house that night. We were supposed to do it weeks ago, but then it got rescheduled."

Several seconds passed with no response.

Fern checked the phone's readout to make sure they were still connected. "Cam?"

"I bet your father wouldn't have any objections to you dating Ted Dees," he said finally, a hint of bitterness in his tone. "Class president. Quarterback. Every parent's dream boy."

"Cam—"

"Let me tell you, beneath that slick surface, he's far from perfect," Cam continued. "You're much safer with me."

"It doesn't matter what the guy is like. Or if my father likes him better." Fern slid back into the warm water, feeling it close around her like a caress. "I already have a boyfriend and he's the one I want."

"You're the one I want, too," Cam said. For a second Fern swore his voice had cracked, but when he spoke again his tone was strong. "You know there's nothing stopping us from going out later on Thursday, after you get back from the dinner."

Nothing except my dad.

"No, there's not," she said.

"Just let me know when you're on your way home and I'll be waiting."

"Cool." Fern found herself pleased with his take-charge attitude. Not to mention she liked knowing she wasn't the only one who didn't want to wait until Friday to get together.

"While I'm gone I'll call or text you every day," Cam promised.

The warmth rushing through Fern had little to do with the steamy bathwater. "I'd like that."

Though Cam didn't say a word, Fern swore she could hear him smiling.

"I suppose I should hang up and go talk to Marcee," he said reluctantly. "She knocked on my door earlier but I told her I'd come down later."

"Tell her hello from me," Fern said. "And Cam . . ."

"Yes, Fern?"

"Will you still be in my back pocket even when you're in Chicago?"

"Is the sky blue?"

"Sam McKelvey is a jerk," Cam said to Marcee, the tips of his ears turning a bright red. "Who does he think he is, telling Fern she can't see me?"

Marcee took a sip of tea and gazed at Cam across the dining room table. When he'd finally come down from his bedroom, she listened eagerly to his account of Fern's encounter with Sam.

Hearing that he'd listened to Fern's side was a huge relief. While she wasn't happy that Sam still seemed to blame her brother for something that was no one's fault, she wasn't worried.

"Sam isn't a jerk," she said with confidence, knowing Cam was stressed over nothing. The way Sam had responded to Fern showed he was a reasonable man. Given time, he would come around on this issue with Cam, too. "He's just being an overprotective father. You have to realize that he's new at this full-time parenting thing."

Cam looked at her in disbelief, then his lip curled. "Why doesn't it surprise me that you're siding with him?"

Marcee drew up in her seat, startled by the venom in his voice. "What do you mean by that?"

"You're screwing him," Cam said flatly. "It only figures you'd take his side."

Marcee's heart fluttered in her chest. She opened her mouth, not sure what to say.

"Don't bother denying it," Cam said. "I saw him leaving here in the middle of the night."

While it didn't particularly bother her that Cam knew she'd been sleeping with Sam, she knew that Sam would be very upset if his daughter found out. "Does Fern know?" she asked.

Cam shook his head, and Marcee breathed a sigh of relief.

"You're not planning to tell her, are you?" Marcee tried her best to sound nonchalant.

"How long has it been going on?"

"We first hooked up in Chicago," she said. "Before I moved here."

Though she wasn't sure how much to divulge, she hoped if she answered some of his questions it would assuage his curiosity so they wouldn't have to discuss it again.

Cam took a sip of soda and eyed Marcee over the top of the can. "So you his girlfriend or what?"

Marcee hesitated. "It's complicated."

Complicated sounded better than saying she had no idea.

Cam lifted a brow. "How so?"

Her brother's anger seemed to have subsided, with natural curiosity taking its place. There was no judgment in his eyes, and Marcee got the feeling there was nothing she could say that would shock him.

"We met at Jenny Carman's wedding reception." Even now Marcee's heart quickened at the memory of that mind-blowing night. "Talked for a while at the reception, then he came up to my room. One night. That's all it was supposed to be."

Thankfully, Cam didn't appear shocked. He merely took another sip of soda and nodded, indicating she still had his attention.

Marcee gave a little laugh. "Then I came here and discovered he was your neighbor."

"You never said you knew him." Cam's tone turned accusatory.

"We decided to keep that fact quiet," Marcee said. "Sam's job is high profile. Neither of us wanted the gossip. Besides, we weren't dating, not really."

"No wonder you were pissed off at the barbecue." Cam pushed back the chair, rose and headed to the cupboard. Only after he was back in his seat with a box of Pop-Tarts sitting in front of him did he finish the thought. "He sleeps with you, yet Mrs. Dees is the one he asks out."

Though Cam had it wrong, the image he painted still rankled. "*She* asked *him* to dinner."

Cam rolled his eyes. "She asked. He accepted."

The same thought had crossed Marcee's mind a time or two, but Sam had explained that he was only going to Paula's house for Fern. But of course that wasn't something she wanted to mention to Cam, not when he'd finally started to chill out.

"Sam asked me to go out with him for breakfast," Marcee pointed out instead. "In the church lobby. Can't get more public than that."

"We both know that was Fern's idea," Cam said, not giving an inch. "And when Mrs. Dees stopped by, he certainly didn't act like you were anything more than just a neighbor."

"I told you. We wanted to keep our relationship just between us." A hint of exasperation—or was it defensiveness?—entered Marcee's tone. "Besides, he *has* taken me out."

Whether it was pride or just plain foolishness, Marcee spent several minutes telling him about the trails they'd walked and the "beach" they'd explored. Not surprisingly, Cam was familiar with the place.

"It's isolated," Cam said. "No one saw you, did they?"

Reluctantly, Marcee shook her head. A heavy weight settled on her chest. She hated doubt.

"Did you stop anywhere afterward?" Cam asked. "Wait, I bet I can answer that. He always took you straight home."

Marcee shifted in her seat, remembering how easily Sam had brushed aside her suggestion that they stop for a quick beer. "We were hot and sweaty, and he had something more romantic in mind anyway."

Cam shook his head. A pitying look filled his gaze. "Why do you do this?"

Marcee's heart rose to her throat.

"You just keep lying to yourself," he said. "You're his booty call. Nothing more. But I'm telling you, if you don't respect yourself, he's never going to either. I think respect is what you want. I know it's what you deserve."

She wanted to tell her brother he was way off base. But the words wouldn't come because he was right about one thing. Sex wasn't all she wanted . . . not with Sam. She wanted to wake up next to him every morning. Share her hopes and dreams with him and have him share hers. She wanted to be his friend. His lover. His . . . wife.

Her heart flip-flopped at the realization that the thought of being married no longer scared her.

"My not sleeping with Sam isn't going to make him respect me," she said finally.

"No," Cam said, his eyes clear and very, very green. "But it'd be a good start."

Sam stared at the computer screen in his office, the events of the past three days running like a DVD in his mind. On Sunday night, just after his discussion with Fern, he'd received a call from dispatch. There had been a pile-up on the highway and another officer was needed.

By the time he got home, Fern was in bed and the lights next door were dark. In a way, he'd been relieved. He couldn't dismiss the nagging feeling that ordering Fern not to see Cam had been too harsh. After all, she was right. If taking the picture frame had been a simple mistake, no one was at fault.

He'd desperately needed to bounce his tangled thoughts off Marcee, and he called her first thing in the morning. She seemed happy to hear that things with Fern had gone well but was uncharacteristically reserved.

At first he'd been concerned about the stay-away-from-me vibes. But if she'd heard what he said to Fern about Cam, she didn't bring it up. When she yawned and mentioned she'd been up late, he decided that was the reason she was being so standoffish. He never felt much like talking when he was tired, either.

That was two days ago. Fern had been staying up extra late, and while Marcee and he had talked on the phone every night, he hadn't seen her since.

Though he'd gone several days before without seeing Marcee, this time it was especially hard. Perhaps he'd knock off early today, he thought, and surprise her with some flowers.

Before he could do more than consider the thought, his door swung open and Ron strolled into the office. The deputy plopped down in the chair in front of Sam's desk.

"I'm a mind-reader," Ron said without preamble.

"You are?" Sam knew he shouldn't encourage the guy, but how else did one respond to such a comment?

"I saw you staring at that monitor, and ol' Ron here knew just what you were thinking." Ron leaned back in the chair and laced his fingers behind his head. "Yep, you're thinkin' about your big date with Paula tomorrow night."

Sam stifled a groan. He'd been thinking about a woman, all right. But it sure hadn't been Paula.

"It's dinner with our families," Sam said, "not a date."

Ron chuckled. "Dorothy Applebee told me about running into the two of you at Grateful Bread. Doesn't sound like just friends to me."

Sam opened his mouth but shut it without speaking. Mentioning that Marcee and Cam had also been there would only be asking for trouble. "Isn't there somewhere you need to be?"

Ron glanced at the clock and a surprised look crossed his face. "Is it really that late?"

Sam nodded.

Ron pushed himself up from the chair. "I'm going out to the woods. Heard some rumblings about a big party in the works."

Sam didn't care where the deputy patrolled, he

was just grateful Ron was headed *somewhere*. He followed Ron into the hall.

"I like to keep one step ahead of the kids," Ron added. "That ain't always easy."

Sam thought about how Fern had him going in circles most days. He sighed. "Ain't that the truth."

*Marcee had just gotten home from the East-*side Nursery when there was a knock at the kitchen door. Even before she pushed back her chair and stood, she knew it would be Sam. He was the only one who ever used the back door.

For a second she thought about not answering, unsure if she could withstand the temptation. For her, Sam was a powerful aphrodisiac, impossible to resist.

She grimaced at the weakness implied in the thought and reworded it . . . *almost* impossible.

Squaring her shoulders, she headed into the

kitchen. Sam smiled through the glass and her traitorous heart skipped a beat.

While she'd given Cam a good overview of her relationship with Sam, she hadn't mentioned the most important fact: she loved the guy. And though she would never say it to anyone, she had the feeling he might love her, too. But now she realized that was just wishful thinking.

Over the past couple of days she had analyzed everything he'd said and done. There was only one conclusion.

If Sam loved her, he'd *want* people to know how he felt. He'd shout it from the rooftops. He definitely wouldn't keep it a secret.

So where did that put their relationship? Feeling unsure of herself and hating the emotion, Marcee fixed a smile on her face, unlocked the door and pulled it open. "This is a surprise."

"Hello, beautiful," Sam said in a deep sexy voice. "I brought you flowers."

She took the bouquet of Gerber daisies and stepped aside to let him pass while breathing in the clean, fresh scent of him. His hair curled against his neck and she fought the urge to slide her fingers through it. Flowers *and* sex appeal. Why couldn't the man fight fair?

"Thank you, Sam." She stared down at the

brightly colored petals of her favorite flower and a lump rose to her throat. "They're beautiful."

"I've missed you, Red," he said.

I've missed you, too. Marcee clamped her lips together, refusing to say the words. She'd vowed she wasn't going to sleep with him again until she knew she had his respect, and she meant to keep that promise. That meant giving him zero encouragement.

But dear God, she'd underestimated the pull, the desire that flashed through her like a raging fire. Her head was telling her to stay strong but her body was staging a major rebellion.

And it wasn't just physical need that tempted her, it was the connection she felt, the closeness she'd had with this man that she feared she would never have again.

You might have felt a connection, but he never did, a voice inside her head jeered. *He doesn't care about you.*

Thankfully, this time her body heard. When Sam reached out, Marcee took a step back. "Want something to drink?"

He raised a brow before a smile lifted the corner of his mouth. "I'll take a beer . . . if you have one."

After placing the daisies in a funky glass vase she'd purchased at a yard sale last week, Marcee slipped past Sam and opened the refrigerator door. For several seconds she let the cold air wash over her, one hand wrapped around the shiny silver can, the green bracelet firmly in sight.

It didn't take long until she felt strong and back in control. She would *not* be any man's booty call.

Grabbing two beers, Marcee turned and found Sam standing . . . right . . . there. She shoved a can at his chest and took a step back.

Popping the tab on hers, she took a long drink. "What's Fern doing tonight?"

"Spending the night with her aunt," Sam said, moving forward, crowding her. "How 'bout Cam?"

"He's in Chicago at a symphony event." Her body hummed from his nearness, but thankfully her voice didn't waiver. "He'll be back tomorrow."

Sam took the can from her hand and placed it along with his on the counter. "You know what that means." His eyes glittered in the fluorescent light. "No chaperones."

Marcee's mouth went dry as her imagination soared. A whole evening with just Sam. Talking . . . laughing . . . loving. Not to mention the fantasies they could explore without interruption . . .

No, she told herself, *no more fantasies*.

"Do you have plans for the evening?" The

heated look he shot her told her that if she didn't, he certainly did.

Twenty-four hours ago the possibility of a whole night of pleasure with this man would have thrilled her. But that was before she'd come to her senses.

"You know," Sam continued, his eyes dark with emotion. "What we've shared these past few weeks has been . . . magical."

Magical. A word normally reserved for story books with happily-ever-after endings.

"You are an amazing woman." Despite having no encouragement, Sam continued. "For you, obstacles are just challenges."

Warmth spread all the way to the tips of her toes at the unsolicited praise. She had received lots of compliments through the years, most centered on her pretty face or sexy body. Yet Sam's words touched her in a way none of the other compliments ever had.

"And despite how you've been treated by your own family, you're a caring, compassionate person," he continued. "The lost child at the wedding. Your brother. The advice on dealing with Fern. Right on target."

That wasn't just desire lurking in Sam's golden depths, there was admiration as well.

Cam had been wrong, she realized with sudden insight. He hadn't understood the depth of the relationship she and this wonderful man shared.

Impulsively, Marcee leaned close and ran her fingers through Sam's soft wavy hair, wondering how she could have ever thought he didn't respect her.

An irritating buzz sounded but Marcee ignored it. They might have all night but she wanted him now. Wanted all of him.

Her fingers fumbled with his belt buckle but Sam's hand closed over hers. "Someone is at the door."

Marcee listened as another buzz sounded. "Ignore it. They'll go away." She grabbed Sam's shirt and pulled it from his waistband just as the buzz sounded again. And then again.

"Damn," Sam muttered.

Marcee paused and looked up just as another buzz sounded.

"They aren't going away," Sam said, frustration in his voice.

Marcee bit back an expletive. The blasted buzzing was screwing with the mood, and the quicker she squelched it, the better.

"I'll get rid of whoever it is," she promised. "Don't go away."

Sam winked. "As if."

After getting one more kiss, Marcee headed to the front door, her irritation rising. There were a plethora of door-to-door salespeople in Ellwood. While she knew they were only trying to earn a living, they needed to understand the three-rings-max rule. If someone doesn't answer in three rings, move on to another house.

She unlocked the front door and jerked it open. "Don't—"

The words died on her lips at the sight of Paula Dees standing on the porch.

"Marcee." Paula's smile widened. "I'm happy I caught you at home. I brought cinnamon rolls."

Marcee stared at the plate Paula shoved into her hands. "Th-Thank you."

"Consider it a belated welcome-back-to-Ellwood gift," Paula said. "They're delicious if I do say so myself."

A distant crack of thunder punctuated her words, followed by a gust of wind so strong it rustled the cellophane covering the rolls and whipped Paula's hair across her face. Drops of rain splattered the porch.

"Where are my manners? Please come inside." Marcee pushed the door open wider and motioned Paula forward.

The woman hesitated. "I don't want to intrude—"

"You aren't. Not at all." After all, no one was naked. No reason for either she or Sam to be embarrassed by an unexpected guest.

Marcee closed the door then led the way down the hall to the kitchen.

"When Fern was talking about cinnamon rolls, it got me in the mood to make some myself," Paula said.

"I'm happy you stopped by, Paula." Marcee spoke loudly, to let Sam know she wasn't alone.

She turned into the kitchen and came to an abrupt halt, startled to find the room empty.

Paula peered over her shoulder. "Something wrong?"

"Not at all." Marcee moved forward, placing the plate on the table. "Would you like something to drink? I've got soda and beer. Or I can make coffee?"

Paula shook her head. "I can't stay long. I'm making brisket for Fern and Sam tomorrow. I still have to stop at the store for a couple items once I leave here."

"Speaking of Sam . . . " Marcee paused, waiting for him to show his face.

"Yes?"

"I saw him today." She improvised even as her heart sank. Where had he gone? "Apparently, Fern's aunt was in town."

"Sam is such a nice guy." Paula's gaze settled on the vase. "What lovely flowers."

"They were a gift," Marcee said without thinking.

Paula's eyes gleamed. "Looks like you have an admirer. Anyone I know?"

The question echoed in the empty room.

"No one who matters," Marcee said. "No one at all."

When Sam heard two sets of footsteps coming down the hall, he grabbed his beer from the counter and slipped through a side door into a back pantry. He'd briefly considered staying put but didn't want to make it awkward for Marcee.

The thought of having his relationship with her become the subject of idle speculation was abhorrent. Even when he was married he'd done his best to keep his personal life private.

That's why he now sat on a step stool in a room no bigger than a walk-in closet. He took a sip of beer, savoring the taste on his tongue. He closed his eyes, remembering the look of pleasure on Marcee's face when he'd given her the flowers.

He was going to have to do that more often . . .

The door to the storage room swung open and slammed against a box. Sam sprang to his feet.

"So this is where you've been hiding," Marcee said, her eyes a cool green.

Sam took a sip of beer and gestured around the room. "Home sweet home."

He expected Marcee to smile but her lips didn't even twitch. "Who was at the door?"

"Paula Dees," Marcee said. "She brought over cinnamon rolls. And asked me if I wanted to go to lunch next week."

"That was nice of her," he said. "Are you going to go?"

"Definitely," Marcee said firmly. "I'm tired of spending so much time alone. Or with Cam."

Sam crossed the room. "You won't be alone tonight."

He leaned over to kiss her but she stiffened and turned her face away. Sam couldn't hide his surprise or his dismay. She'd been on fire less than fifteen minutes earlier. Now she was so cold he could feel the chill just standing next to her. "What's wrong?"

"I'm hungry." Marcee lifted her chin. "The Coffee Pot has all-you-can-eat fish on Wednesdays. Want to go?"

The last place Sam wanted to go was the popular downtown café. He had no doubt everyone and anyone looking for a good deal would be there. It would be crowded and noisy and he wouldn't even have a chance to enjoy Marcee's company.

"Not really," he said with what he hoped was an engaging smile. "I'd rather stay here and have you all to myself. I'm sure we can find something to tempt our taste buds here."

Marcee tilted her head and her gaze turned speculative. "Do you realize you've never come through my front door?"

She'd shifted direction again, and he was finding it difficult to track. "So I use the back door. Is that a problem?"

"You don't want anyone to know you're sleeping with me."

"Of course I don't," Sam said promptly, wondering where she was going with this.

"Why?"

Did he need to spell it out again? By the tight set to her jaw, apparently he did.

"Because of Fern mostly. And because I don't like to feed the gossip mill." If talk arose, Fern would hear it . . . and possibly be hurt by it. "You need to understand—"

"I understand," Marcee said between clenched

lips. "You don't want to *date* me. You just want to *fuck* me."

"We do not *fuck*," Sam said between gritted teeth, finding the word and its implication totally offensive. "We *make love*."

Marcee's gaze locked with his for a long moment. "To make love you have to love the other person." She lifted her chin. "It doesn't matter what you call it. I'm tired of being your booty call."

"What are you talking about? That's not how it is at all," Sam said vehemently, his heart twisting at the look of sadness in her eyes.

Dear God, he'd done what he had sworn never to do—he'd hurt her. An overwhelming urge to take her in his arms and make her realize how much she meant to him washed over him. He wanted nothing more than to promise her not only his nights, but his days as well.

But hard as it was, he kept his hands at his side. He'd let his own needs, his own desires, come before Fern's welfare for too many years. Now that he had the chance to make up for the mistake, he wouldn't blow it. "If I could give you more I would."

"You can," Marcee said. "You just don't want to."

Before he could respond, she turned and headed back into the kitchen, leaving him no choice but to trail behind her. He followed her down the hall, all the way to the front door.

A sick feeling filled Sam's stomach. When she pulled open the door and gestured for him to leave, panic raced through his veins. He couldn't lose her.

"C'mon, Marcee," he said, hating the desperation in his tone. "We have something special."

"It was a fling. Nothing more. And now it's over." A curtain seemed to drop over her expression. "My light is officially off."

Paula smiled at Sam across her dining room table. "I made your favorite pie for dessert, sour cream apple."

"Sounds wonderful." Sam returned the smile, resisting the urge to glance at his watch. Although dinner had been delicious, all he'd been able to think about was Marcee.

When he'd gone to her house last night, he never expected her to . . . well . . . break up with him. He told himself he should have expected it. After all, what they'd shared was *supposed* to be

just temporary. But dammit, it hadn't felt temporary. His feelings had been real. Deep.

Sam sighed and returned his attention to his
hostess, hoping he could continue to listen rather
than talk. Thankfully, Ted seemed more than willing to carry the conversation. Throughout dinner he'd heard all about Ted's latest awards and
about the colleges interested in having him sign a
football letter of intent.

Fern made an attempt to contribute, but Ted
seemed determined to monopolize the conversation. While the boy was a bit too cocky for Sam's
liking, he had to admit that Ted had a lot going for
him. At least, according to Ted.

"Some of my friends are getting together at the
community center this evening," Ted said, turning to Fern. "If you're interested in coming with
me, I'd be happy to introduce you around."

Fern's eyes brightened. "The community center
by my house?"

"There's only one," Ted said with a laugh.

Disappointment crossed Paula's face. "What
about dessert?"

"I don't want any," Ted said, pushing back his
chair. "C'mon, Fern, it's time to boogie."

Fern rose to her feet and smiled at Paula. "Dinner was delicious, Mrs. Dees. Thank you for inviting me."

"Don't be too late," Sam said.

"I won't," Fern said, wiggling her fingers good-bye.

Once Ted and Fern left, Paula's youngest headed upstairs to play a video game, leaving Sam and Paula alone.

If Sam could have found a way to leave, he'd have been out the door, too. But Paula had gone to a lot of trouble to make the evening nice so he ended up agreeing to dessert. Instead of eating at the table, Paula suggested they have their coffee and pie in the family room.

By the time Sam finished his piece, the conversation had hit a lull. He and Marcee never ran out of things to say, he thought with a pang.

"I stopped over at your neighbor's house last night and dropped off some cinnamon rolls," Paula said after a particularly long silence. "I've been on a baking frenzy the past couple days."

She chuckled even as her expression grew pensive. "I hate to think what it's going to be like once the boys are grown. Who am I going to cook and bake for then?"

Her gaze lingered on Sam, and the interest in

her eyes sent red flags popping up. Perhaps Ron wasn't the only one who'd thought tonight was more than a simple get-together.

"You're doing the right thing," Sam said. "Making them your priority now."

The minute the words left his mouth, Sam wondered who he was trying to convince.

"Am I?" Paula's lips twisted. "Sometimes I'm not so sure."

"Think about it." He leaned forward, resting his forearms on his legs. "If you were involved with someone, the boys would get shortchanged."

Paula's expression turned doubtful. She shook her head. "I think that happens more when children are small, rather than this age. I don't know about Fern, but most of the time my sons would rather hang out with their friends than spend time with me."

"You may be right," Sam grudgingly admitted, "but at least you're available when they *are* around."

Paula gazed at him over the top of her china cup. "Personally, I think it would be good for the boys—and for Fern as well—to see their parent dating. For them to know that I—or you, for example—were still capable of having a loving, meaningful relationship."

It was an interesting argument, made even more compelling by the fact that Paula was also a single parent. "Would you ever consider marrying again?" he asked.

"I would." Paula placed her cup in the saucer. "Assuming I found the right man. Of course, there are quite a few things I'd do differently this time around."

Sam tilted his head, surprised at her candor. "I thought you and your husband had a good relationship."

"We did." Paula nodded for extra emphasis. "But it certainly wasn't perfect." She gave a little laugh. "Then again, what marriage is?"

"In the past, my career came before my marriage, before my family," Sam found himself admitting. "What's to stop me from making that mistake again?"

"My guess is that your wife didn't force the issue."

Sam thought back to those days. "Laura was very understanding."

"Enabling."

Sam's head jerked up. "What?"

"Sounds like instead of calling you on your behavior, she let you get away with it," Paula said matter-of-factly. "That doesn't in any way excuse you. But if she'd stood up to you, things may have been different."

Sam straightened in his chair, not liking the direction of this conversation or Paula's insinuation. "My wife wasn't a doormat, if that's what you're implying."

As if realizing she may have pushed too hard, Paula leaned over and squeezed his hand. "I didn't mean any disrespect. Goodness, if anyone can identify with her, it's me. Jake had a strong personality and I let him run the show, rather than being a true partner. All I was trying to say is if I were given another chance, I'd do a lot of things differently."

Sam thought of Laura. Of Fern. And Marcee. He'd made so many mistakes. He couldn't change what had happened with Laura, but hopefully he still had time to make it up to Fern and Marcee.

He sure as hell was going to give it his best.

Sam got to the woods shortly after nine. When Ron had called for backup—apologizing all over himself for interrupting Sam's evening with Paula—it gave Sam the excuse he'd needed to cut the evening short.

He could tell Paula was disappointed, but even if he hadn't been alerted to trouble, he would have still left. Staying longer would have only given her false hope. Though she was a nice woman, he just wasn't interested.

He'd stopped at home to change into his uniform and then headed straight to the woods. There were at least thirty kids still needing to be ticketed for alcohol possession when he arrived.

He recognized one of them immediately. "Ted," he called out, motioning the boy over. "What are you doing here? I thought you were going to the community center."

Ted sauntered over. "No one cool goes to the community center."

"They don't get cited for MIP either." Sam kept his voice level, despite the fact that the boy's attitude had started to grate on him.

Surprise crossed Ted's face. "You're not really going to ticket me."

Sam held up his pad. "Just as soon as I get it written out." He glanced around. "Where's Fern?"

"She split right after we got here," Ted said. "Apparently partying with the cool crowd isn't *her thing*."

Ted's tone made it clear what he thought of *that* attitude. But Sam had more important things on his mind than the kid's arrogance . . . his daughter's welfare, for one thing.

"How could she go anywhere?" Sam demanded. "She didn't have a car."

"She called someone." Ted shrugged. "A red-headed dude picked her up."

Sam narrowed his gaze. "Camden Smith?"

"I guess that's his name," Ted said. "He's not someone I hang with."

"Thank God," Sam muttered. He quickly finished the ticket and handed it to the boy. "Sign this."

Why had he ever hoped that Fern and this boy would be friends? It was just one more lapse in judgment. One more mistaken first impression.

Just like when he'd immediately dismissed Cam, the honor roll student who performed with the symphony in Chicago. Or when he'd walked away from Marcee, telling himself that it was because he needed to give Fern all his time and attention.

The truth, he now realized, was that he'd been afraid of hurting another woman like he hurt Laura. He hadn't been that good a husband the first time around and worried that he might repeat those same mistakes.

Talking to Paula had brought those fears to the surface. But he'd also experienced a freeing realization. The past did not determine the future.

Marcee would never let him ignore her. He had no doubt she would kick his butt if he deserved it.

Now that he knew where he'd gone wrong, he hoped it wasn't too late to make it right.

"Are you sure you want to do this?" Cam spoke in a low whisper even though the street in front of Fern's house was deserted.

Fern tightened her hold on his hand and pulled him up the front steps. "I refuse to sneak around."

Just saying the words bolstered her courage.

"Your dad told you not to see me again," Cam reminded her. "This is like throwing me in his face."

"He needs to know you're not going away—" Fern yelped as the front door abruptly swung open.

"I've been waiting for you two." A grim-faced Sam held the door open and stepped aside to let them enter.

Cam tried to let go of her hand but Fern held on tight.

"I suppose," Fern said to her father once they were inside, "you're wondering what happened to Ted."

"Let's talk in the living room." Sam turned and walked down the hall. "It's more comfortable in there."

Fern smiled reassuringly at Cam. That little muscle in her father's jaw always jumped when he was upset. The fact that it hadn't made an appearance was a good sign.

After taking a seat on the sofa, she pulled Cam down next to her. Her dad settled himself into his favorite chair.

"I—" Sam began.

"Before you say anything," Fern said quickly. "You need to know that *I* called Cam. He—"

"I'm glad you did."

For a second Fern was sure she'd misunderstood. "Say what?"

Her father shifted his gaze to Cam. "Thank you for picking her up and bringing her home. I appreciate it."

"Ted didn't take me to the community center, Dad. He took me to the woods," Fern said. "I told him I didn't want to go but he wouldn't listen to me—"

"I heard what happened." Sam rubbed a hand across his face. "I was wrong to push Ted on you. Especially when all I knew about him was what a few adults told me."

Cam shot Fern an I-told-you-so look and Fern smiled.

"Camden, I don't particularly like your hair." Sam's words wiped the smile from Fern's face. "And I sure as hell don't like the ring in your brow."

Fern opened her mouth to protest but Cam squeezed her hand and shook his head.

"But from everything I've seen, you appear to be a good kid." Sam's mouth twisted. "Plus, my daughter thinks a lot of you and I'm learning to trust her judgment."

"Why the change?" Fern couldn't figure it out. "Was it because you found out Ted is a jerk?"

Next to her, Cam stifled a chuckle.

"The truth is I'd have had a problem with *any* boy," Sam said. "I know now that I have to accept the fact that you're a young lady, not my little girl."

Tears welled in Fern's eyes but she quickly blinked them back. "I'll always be your little girl."

"I'll never hurt your daughter," Cam said, his arm sliding around Fern's shoulders.

Her father gazed at Cam for a long moment, and to Fern it was almost as if he was seeing him for the first time. Then he smiled. "I'll hold you to that promise."

With those words, Sam rose to his feet. "Now if you'll excuse me, there's someone else who deserves an apology."

Though it was barely past midnight, Marcee had already taken a shower and scrubbed off her makeup. She'd just finished slathering on antiaging lotion when the doorbell buzzed.

She grabbed her silk robe and pulled it over her chemise on her way to the front door, trying to still her rising irritation. It was the third time this week that Cam had forgotten his house key.

She jerked open the door. "Next time you forget—"

The rest of the threat died on her lips at the sight of Sam—in uniform—on her porch. His face was tense and his shoulders as stiff as any soldier. A chill traveled up her spine.

"Is Camden okay?" Marcee glanced around him, her fear growing when she realized Sam was alone. Cam had left the house shortly after nine, promising to be home by midnight. "Was he—has there been an accident?"

A knot formed in the pit of her stomach.

Dear God, why had she let Cam leave the house without knowing where he was going? He'd mentioned a friend who needed a ride—but she hadn't even asked who or where. What kind of mother—er, sister—was she?

"Camden is fine," Sam said quickly. "Actually, he's at my house. Fern just stuck in a movie when I left."

Marcee leaned back against the door frame, her knees weak. "I saw you in that uniform and imagined all sorts of horrible things."

Sam glanced down, and when he looked up, she could see the apology in his eyes. "I didn't realize I still had this on. I didn't mean to frighten you."

"Thanks for letting me know Cam is at your house. But next time, just tell him to call."

She started to push the door shut, but Sam's foot shot out and stopped it. "I didn't come to talk about your brother," he said. "I came to talk about us."

Her heart began to race but she immediately brought it under control. "There is no *us*," she said. "There's just you and me. And *you* need to leave . . . before *me* calls the cops."

"You forget," Sam said lightly, that blasted dimple flashing in his cheek. "In this town I am the police."

"I haven't forgotten *anything*," Marcee said, fighting off the attraction that still raged between them.

"C'mon, Red." His gaze met hers, and her insides tensed and melted at the same time. "Let me come in. I want to set things right between us."

Marcee steeled herself against the desire to let him in, to believe anything and everything he had to say. "Too late. I'm done listening."

"Let me explain—"

"Didn't anyone ever tell you," she said, putting her hand on his chest and shoving him back, hard, "that actions speak louder than words?"

23

For a Saturday, the tiny bistro just off Mich-
igan Avenue was surprisingly empty. When Marcee called and told Jenny to choose where they
would meet for lunch, Jenny suggested a place
she and Robert often ate.

"I was so happy to hear your voice," Jenny said,
forking off a piece of her quiche. "It seems like
forever since we just sat and talked."

Marcee smiled. While she liked Jenny and had
missed seeing her, today she wasn't into gabbing
as much as just keeping herself busy. Since Thursday, she'd made a concerted effort to fill her days
. . . and evenings.

Friday, she and Cam had spent the entire day in Chicago at an electronics trade show. She tried to get him to go to dinner with her afterward, but he'd already made plans with Fern.

Since the last thing she wanted was to spend the night alone, she'd called Iris and Paula and the three of them had gone clubbing in Chicago.

But Paula hadn't been with them long. They'd run into Jeff and some friends early in the evening. Marcee was shocked to see him until she learned that Paula had spoken with him earlier in the day. He clearly had a thing for Paula, and when he asked her if she'd like to check out a new martini bar downtown, Iris and Marcee had sent her off with their blessing.

Iris had spent most of the evening flirting with a Denzel look-alike, and she . . . well, there had been lots of men, paying her all sorts of compliments and showering her with attention. All hoping for a no strings night of fun. But she wanted someone who cared about *her*, not just about her body. Oh, heck, who was she kidding? She wanted Sam. She loved Sam. And if he'd only loved her back, everything—

The pressure of a hand over hers jerked Marcee back to the present. She looked up to find Jenny staring, her blond brows pulled together in concern. "Is there something you're not telling me?"

Marcee gave a little laugh and straightened in her seat. "What makes you think that?"

"Well, for starters, you haven't heard a word I've said in the last five minutes. And," Jenny leaned forward and lowered her voice to a confidential whisper, "you haven't given those two men over there a single glance."

Marcee shifted her gaze to the right. The men were in their mid-thirties, with full heads of hair and good builds. The guy with sandy brown hair wore a wedding ring, but the dark-haired one's ring finger was bare. He caught her staring and smiled, showing a mouthful of perfect white teeth.

Marcee turned back to Jenny. "Not my type."

Jenny laughed. "Since when?"

"Since I went all stupid and fell in love with Sam McKelvey." There, she'd said it.

"Fern's dad?" The surprise in Jenny's eyes was quickly replaced with delight. "Why . . . that's wonderful. You never told me the two of you were dating."

"We aren't—weren't—dating." Marcee pushed her plate of food aside. "We were just having sex. But we're not even doing that now."

The delight in Jenny's eyes turned to puzzlement. "I'm totally confused."

"It's not that difficult to understand," Marcee said. "We had an itch. We scratched it."

"You said you loved him," Jenny reminded her.

Marcee wasn't sure how to respond to that honestly without looking like a fool. Thankfully, the waitress chose that moment to stop and inquire about dessert.

"I'll have crème brulée and an espresso." Marcee shifted her gaze to Jenny.

"Just a cappuccino for me, please," Jenny said.

The waitress had barely stepped away from the table when Marcee resumed conversing, but changed the subject. "Tell me about your new house." She knew there was nothing Jenny liked to talk about more than the house she and her husband were having built. "Did you end up going with a marble floor in the foyer?"

"Good try." Jenny's lips quirked upward. "But the only thing we're going to talk about is you. Specifically, what's going on between you and Sam McKelvey."

"Don't you understand, there is no me and Sam. Not anymore—" To Marcee's horror, her voice broke. She blinked rapidly and clamped her lips together. Her friend was gracious enough not to press her while she regained her composure.

"Tell me what happened," Jenny said after the waitress brought them their drinks and dessert and then departed. Her tone was soft and low, inviting confidences. "If anyone will understand what you're going through, it's me."

"Apparently, I'm not good enough for him." Marcee fixed her gaze on her crème brulée, unable to meet Jenny's gaze.

"He said that?" Jenny's voice rose, the simmering anger in her tone warming Marcee's heart. "To think I always liked the guy," she continued, disappointment on her face. "I mean, I didn't know him well, but he was always nice to my family."

Though a part of Marcee wanted to fuel Jenny's anger, her mature side—the part she was trying to cultivate—insisted she tell her friend the whole story. So she took a deep breath and started at the beginning, when she'd first seen Sam at the reception, ending with her slamming the door in his face Thursday night.

Jenny looked toward the ceiling. "I don't know what to say."

Marcee took another sip of espresso, the bitter

taste matching her mood. "You don't have to say anything."

"There's something I must be missing," Jenny said slowly, and Marcee could almost see the wheels turning in her friend's analytical mind. "It doesn't sound like he was ashamed of you. It sounds more like he didn't want Fern to find out the two of you were . . . involved."

"Same thing."

"Ummm, not really." Jenny shook her head. "Most parents go to great lengths to keep their sex lives private from their children."

Marcee felt a chill travel all the way to her toes. Jenny was her best friend, the one she'd been sure she could count on. "You're siding with him."

"You know better than that," Jenny said, sounding offended. Still, her expression remained pensive. "Maybe it's just because I can identify with Sam. I can't help remembering how I felt when Robert wouldn't let *me* explain."

"But he came around," Marcee said gently at the look of distress on her friend's face. "And now you're the happiest married couple I know."

"That's what I'm trying to say." Jenny's voice took on a surprising urgency. "Perhaps you should talk to Sam one more time. See what he has to say. Hear him out."

It sounded so simple. But Jenny didn't understand that the way she felt about Sam made it hard for her to remain objective. "I'm not going to be a fool."

"Don't let pride stand in the way." Jenny gave her hand a quick squeeze. "Before you throw away something special, just be sure you really do have all the answers."

Jenny's words haunted Marcee all the way home. When she awoke the next morning, they were still with her, niggling at her.

She'd planned to skip church, but when Cam told her that Sam and Fern would be attending the evening service, she decided to go. Anything to keep busy. Anything to get her mind off Sam.

The minister spent the whole service talking about forgiveness. For a second Marcee thought he was talking straight to her . . . until she caught Cam casting her sideways glances. She couldn't figure out why until she remembered last night . . . when he'd forgotten his keys . . . again.

She smiled to let him know that she forgave him for being a thoughtless idiot. In spite of her benevolence, Cam still seemed stressed, so when he asked if they could go to the Coffee Pot after church, she quickly agreed.

She had an ulterior motive, of course. Even if Sam went out for lunch, she knew there would be no chance of running into him at the downtown eatery.

When they entered the café, Marcee spotted a booth in the back, but Cam insisted on a table in the center. They'd just gotten their drinks when Cam pushed back his chair and stood.

"Where are you going?" She lifted her gaze from the unfamiliar menu. "The waitress will be back to take our order any minute."

"I, ah, I . . . " Cam hesitated and his ears turned bright red. "I have to go . . . uh . . . to the bathroom."

"Then you'd better go," Marcee said quickly, resisting the urge to smile at his embarrassment. She'd never realized that teenage boys were so sensitive.

Her brother disappeared, and Marcee returned her attention to all the delicious-sounding selections. It wasn't until she heard the chair scrape against the floor that she looked up. But it wasn't Cam seated to her right, it was *Sam*.

"You should be at the Grateful Bread," Marcee said stupidly.

"I had other plans," Sam said. "Hold out your right hand."

"Why?"

"Just do it," he said, then softened the request with a heart-stopping smile. "Please."

Without thinking it through, Marcee held out her hand. Faster than she could say *What the hell?* a band of steel encircled her wrist. And before she could pull away, Sam slapped the other cuff around his.

The waitress who was approaching the table stopped and her eyes widened. Without a word she turned on her heel and scurried back toward the kitchen.

"What do you think you're doing?" Marcee demanded. "What's this about?"

Sam's eyes were dark and intense. "I need to explain and I want to make sure you stay with me long enough to listen."

"This is false imprisonment," Marcee sputtered. "I could have your badge over this."

"I realize that," Sam said quietly, his gaze never leaving hers. "I'm willing to take the risk."

Marcee's breath caught in her throat. For him to put his job on the line, this had to be important. "I suppose I can spare a few minutes."

Out of the corner of her eye Marcee saw Dorothy Applebee, along with several of her friends, watching with unabashed interest. If Sam was worried about the gossipmongers, he couldn't have picked a worse place for a conversation.

"What do you want to say?" Marcee said, hating the trace of belligerence in her tone, but hating even more that she still found herself wanting to believe she'd been wrong about him.

"You're angry with me."

"Not at all." She forced a light, airy tone. "To be angry I'd have to care."

"Well, I care," Sam said, his eyes the color of amber. "I love you."

He spoke so loudly, the customers at nearby tables couldn't help but hear. Knowing the efficiency of the Ellwood grapevine, Marcee had no doubt the declaration would be all over town in less than thirty minutes.

"You don't love me." She kept her voice low. Just because he was acting crazy didn't mean she had to play along. "We both know that."

"Why is that so hard for you to believe?" Sam asked, his gaze lingering on her face. "From the first moment I saw you there was something about you, something special . . . "

Sam continued to extol her virtues, but after a moment Marcee tuned him out. It was too painful . . . hearing the heart-tugging words and wanting to believe them. It was all just talk.

"I've heard all I need to hear." She jerked to her feet and held out her arm. "Unlock this."

Before Sam could respond, Cam appeared out of nowhere. He slid his arm firmly around Marcee's shoulder, holding her captive. "Sit down and let him finish."

He exchanged a look with Sam, and Marcee realized that running into Sam this morning had been no coincidence. She'd been set up by her own brother.

"I'll get you for this," she hissed to Cam.

"I'm sure you will," Cam said with a benign smile. "Now sit."

Marcee dropped back into her seat with a huff. "That's pretty low," she said to Sam as Cam sauntered off. "Using my brother to get to me."

"I was desperate," Sam said, not at all apologetic. "Besides he asked what he could do to help."

"Why would he do that?" Marcee asked. It made no sense. Cam was the one who'd told her to steer clear of Sam.

"I told him how much I loved you," Sam said.

Marcee couldn't hide her surprise. "And he believed you?"

Sam nodded. "He knows I love you. Fern knows I love you."

"Quit saying that," she ordered between gritted

teeth. "You didn't want anyone to know you were seeing me. That doesn't sound like love to me."

"What we had was so special that I didn't want to share it with anyone else," Sam said. "I never stopped to think how it looked, or felt to you. I was wrong and I'm sorry."

The apology sounded sincere but the hurt remained. "Talk is cheap."

"I thought you might say that." Without warning, Sam rose to his feet. "Attention everyone, I have an announcement to make."

He spoke loudly and with so much authority that conversation in the café instantly stopped. "I want you all to know that I'm in love with Marcee Robbens."

With that pronouncement, Sam sat down and turned to her, ignoring the buzzing in the room. "I thought about telling them we'll be getting married, but it seemed that I should ask you first."

The dimple in Sam's cheek flashed and the steel surrounding Marcee's heart began to soften.

"Married?" The word came out of her lips on a squeak.

"I want to spend my life with you." Sam reached over and covered her hand with his. "If you don't want to live in Ellwood, we'll move back to Chicago."

"But what about your job contract?" Marcee wasn't sure, but she thought Paula had said he'd signed a three-year contract with the city.

"I'll break it," he said, and the set of his jaw told her it wasn't an idle statement.

"But if you did that, you might not be able to work in law enforcement again."

"My career isn't the most important thing in my life," he said. "My family—you and Fern—are."

Marcee glanced down at her bracelet. She'd reached high and she'd gotten all she could have wanted and more. A wave of love swamped her, nearly drowning her in its wake, washing away the last of her doubts.

"I haven't told you my news," she said. "I just accepted a job at the Eastside Nursery. I'm their new CFO." She prattled happily, feeling practically giddy. "I think it'll be perfect. I'll take care of the financials but they've also agreed to let me get my hands dirty with the plants as often as I want. I guaranteed them a year. That'll get Cam out of high school. After that, we can reevaluate."

Sam looked dazed, then hope filled his eyes. "Are you saying you accept my proposal?"

"Yes . . . No . . . Maybe." Marcee's head was spinning. "What about Fern? What does she think of all this?"

Sam gestured with his head to a booth where Fern sat cuddled close to Cam. "I think she's hoping that if I'm busy with my own love life, I won't be nosing around in hers as much."

Marcee chuckled. "She still has a lot to learn about her dad."

"You know me so well." Sam smiled.

Marcee's heart warmed as she realized it was true. She did know him. And trust him. And most of all she loved him more than she'd ever thought it was possible to love any man.

"I'm still waiting for an answer," he said.

"Isn't a proposal usually offered up on bended knee?" she teased.

Without a word, Sam slipped from his chair and dropped to one knee.

By the sudden silence surrounding them, Marcee knew she and Sam now had the attention of the entire room. But the other diners weren't important. At this moment all she cared about was the man kneeling before her.

He fumbled for a second in his pocket, finally pulling out a tiny black velvet box. Flipping it open, he took a sparkling diamond solitaire out with trembling fingers.

"Marcee," he said, his heart in his eyes, "I wish

that words could convey the happiness that you've brought to my life. I believe it was destiny that brought us together. You are truly the half that makes me whole. I do not wish any other partner, any other companion, any other wife but you. I can't picture the rest of my life without you by my side. And, I promise you, the light of love in my heart will always be on and whenever you need me I'll be there. Marcee Robbens, will you marry me?"

It wasn't just the words that touched her heart and brought a lump to her throat, it was the tremor in his voice and the unmistakable look of love in his eyes.

"I love you, too," she whispered, realizing she'd never known what love was until she met Sam.

She opened her mouth to tell him just that when Dorothy Applebee shouted from across the room. "We couldn't hear her answer over here. What did she say?"

Marcee met Sam's gaze. It was all there, the love, the devotion, the until-death-do-us-part. Her heart overflowed with love and happiness and she found herself laughing with pure joy.

"What did she say?" Dorothy repeated.

"She says yes," Marcee said loudly enough

for everyone—including Dorothy Applebee—to hear.

And when Sam slid the ring on her finger and the café erupted in applause, she wanted to cheer. Because there wasn't anyone in the world that she'd rather be handcuffed with for eternity than Sam McKelvey.